The Album

The Album

Growing Up in the Age of Innocence

Steven Wilcox

Steven Wilcox

CONTENTS

CONTENTS

Dedicated to my parents and brothers

Bill and Erma

Billy and John

In loving memory of my parents and my brothers

Bill and Erma
Billy, and John

First Printing, 2021

1

In the Beginning

IN THE BEGINNING

Pasadena is at the base of the western-most edge of the San Gabriel Mountains. It was one of the last tracts controlled by a single Mexican national when the United States annexed California. It has been a tourist destination and a stop on the Atchison, Topeka, and the Santa Fe rail line from time to time. Mount Wilson is the tallest peak in the range, and it sits overlooking sprawling Pasadena below. Pasadena has always been a magnet for immigrants, welcoming African Americans and Mexicans following the civil war and Pacific Asians. In 1890, the city celebrated its diverse heritage with a parade welcoming in the new year. I grew up calling it the Rose Parade, but we officially know it as The Tournament of Roses. They finished the now-familiar Rose Bowl in the 1920s, and in 1922, a football game following the parade became a tradition.

My mother's parents were Pennsylvania Dutch and settled in Wilkes-Barre, Pennsylvania. When World War I broke out, my grandfather enlisted and was an ambulance driver. He served with a skinny kid from North Dakota who decorated his ambulance with cartoon caricatures. His name was Walter Elias Disney.

After the war, my grandparents migrated west and settled in Pasadena, where they had five kids: three girls and two boys. He was a masonry contractor. Like most mothers of her day, she was a stay at home mom. Since most homes in California were stucco, he mostly crafted fireplaces and chimneys for residential construction. He enjoyed building things and had a workshop to prove it. He had a table saw, a band saw and taught each of us how to use a coping saw to create projects out of balsa.

Their eldest daughter, Thelma loved music and dancing. She worked at the Ice Palace, a public ice-skating rink in Pasadena. She was the counter clerk, cashier, and skating instructor. She put her love of music and dancing together, teaching her students the art of ice dancing and traditional figure skating.

Working at the Ice Palace was a good-looking guy from neighboring Glendale, with wavy brown hair named Frank Stoneman. Mutt and Jeff was a famous comic strip at this time. It was about two friends, one very tall (Jeff) and one very short (Mutt). Frank was her Jeff, and she was his Mutt. Frank towered over her with his six-one, muscular frame. He had captivating brown eyes, a firm chin, and like her dad, he was always tinkering with things, especially at the ice rink. Thelma, on the other hand, was petite, standing just under five-three. She was pretty and cute and caught the eye of many a guy whose eyesight she crossed. Thelma was positive that Frank did some tinkering so that he could impress her.

Frank was born in Denver, Colorado, and was an only child. Before his fifth birthday, he and his family moved to neighboring Glendale. Frank's dad found a job as a conductor on the Pacific Electric Streetcar Line. Louis Stoneman was short and thin and was known for his engaging smile and sense of humor. Frank got his height from his mother, who was at least six feet tall. While she worked as a cleaning lady for a couple of banks, her first love was making intricate holiday decorations. Her friends were amazed as her fingers were not dainty. Instead of being long and thin, generally associated with her hobby, her fingers were short and thick. Frank would spend hours watching his mother create her masterpieces. Watching her provided him with the desire to build things.

Frank's job at the skating rink was to keep the music playing–literally. He did the installation of the loudspeakers and ensured the music was heard. He selected and played the records for general skating as well as the music Thelma wanted teaching. For special lessons, Thelma and Frank would discuss what music would be appropriate over a cup of hot cocoa. They were falling madly in love.

The two of them dated for a couple of years. Frank would play hooky just to be able to meet her when she got out of school. They would take walks and sit for hours with Thelma's friends at the Woolworth soda counter. They got married and moved to a two-bedroom bungalow on Delores Avenue, about 15 minutes from Thelma's parent's home. The house was white stucco with a Spanish tile roof. Frank had to park on the street since their little bungalow had neither a garage nor a drive-way. Although it was only two blocks from busy Colorado Boulevard, Delores was a quiet street where everyone knew everyone else.

The Roaring Twenties were over, and the depressive thirties were nearing an end. As the thirties gave way to the forties, Hitler was running unchallenged in Europe. Many had a sense of patriotism and did not want Hitler setting his signs across the ocean on the United States. Being on the west coast, seeing many sailors and more than a few ships down at Long Beach, Frank enlisted in the Navy. Frank and Thelma did not have a lot of money and spent most of their time working – at work or around their rent house. They never went to the beach, and Frank never went as a child before meeting Thelma. Had Frank gone to the beach, he would have known that he developed hives from an unusual allergic reaction to the ocean's water. He found this out when he enlisted in the Navy. You can't be in the Navy and be allergic to saltwater, so they cut him loose.

The next day, he enlisted in the Marine Corps. They assured him his saltwater allergy was not a problem with them and welcomed him with open arms – for a day. As it turned out, he had enlisted in the Marines before his discharge from the Navy was complete. So, they let him go as well.

Frank had gotten work pulling wire on new commercial construction and put the idea of military service aside. In December 1942, just days before Pearl Harbor, Thelma presented Frank with his first child. A son they called Earl. Three days after Earl made his appearance, the Japanese bombed the naval base at Pearl Harbor, Hawaii.

Busy with a new child and more work than he could handle, he had forgotten about his military plans. However, Uncle Sam has a long memory and reached out to him in March 1943 and said, "Come, my son, I and your country need you." He would be gone for most of three years.

In those days, there were no such luxuries as garbage disposals. One gathered up food scraps and placed them in a small metal pole with a tight-fitting lid to keep out the critters. Jack and Thelma played hide and seek a lot; it was his favorite game. One day while Thelma was pretending to hide, she heard the back door open and shut as Earl went out presumably to hid. Thelma gave him a minute and then went out to look for her son. There were not many places to hide in that yard, and after three or four minutes without finding him, she called after him.

She was looking in one direction when she heard a noise behind her. The pale in which the food scraps are thrown wobbled and up popped Earl, lid on his head – and some other unsavory items dangling from his hair and clothing – smiling from ear to ear and announced, "Here I are!" From that day forward, Thelma insisted they play hide and seek to be played only indoors. Earl readily agreed as he was not particularly fond of the scrubbing he received at bath time, which had been moved up from after dinner to as soon as they were in the house.

Frank served in the Pacific Campaign and did not talk much of what he saw or did. He showed Thelma the Bronze Star for Heroism he received but never elaborated on how he had earned it. That was in November 1945. Earl was almost three and not sure who this giant was that had moved into their house. By Christmas, however, Earl and the giant were positively inseparable.

On Independence Day, 1946, and one minute past midnight, Thelma welcomed Bruce into the family. Now, as an infant coming into this world, you have no cognitive functions. You are yelling and screaming; you are all wet in a variety of technicolor hues, and you truly have a face that a mother could love. Dad, on the other hand, was not sure exactly what his lovely wife was holding.

"What? You want me to hold that thing?"

"Yes, dear, he's your son and looks just like you," Thelma said reassuringly.

"But I might break it," protested Frank. Still not referring to the bundle he was now holding as human.

"There, see, he likes you." Frank looked down, and whatever it was he was holding; it was both precious, and it was his. He smiled and talked to son number two.

As I said, as an infant, you come into this world unable to speak. Your eyes may be closed, you may or may not have hair (I didn't!), and everything is big, bright, and new. Not even your parents know what to think of you, other than a loving gift from God.

But I was destined to be different. I would be the second of three boys. Earl, and two years after me, Jack would be born at the Pasadena Hospital for Women. I was born at the newer Huntington Memorial Hospital in Pasadena. Like most Southern California, Pasadena lies on a fault line, and earthquakes are frequent and familiar. Most are just a gentle shake of the earth. However, pregnant with Jack and making preparations for another Huntington Memorial birth, an earthquake shook the area bursting a natural gas line outside the hospital, causing extensive fire damage. Most of the hospital sustained minor damage, but they were not accepting new patients. Like his older brother Earl, Jack would arrive via the Pasadena Hospital for Women.

I have had friends insisting God has a plan for us, and whatever happens is part of his plan. I believe our God is a loving father, but he also gave us free will, which means the choices we make determine who we are. One of my favorite movie lines is "You become what you are." God does not dictate our life's path because of free will; he does, however, influence it with the talents he bestowed upon us. Morgan Freeman said that line in *And Along Came a Spider* and explained that God gives us specific talents and all we have to do listen and nurture them. It is those unique talents given to us at conception that make us who we are. What we do with them is up to us.

We are an amalgam of those who bring us up, the experiences we have as children, and our dreams. My mother's family moved from Pennsylvania to California, leaving family and friends behind to strike out to forge a life of their own. My dad's parents moved from Colorado to California with their own dreams. Both families had a sense of adventure and sought to make their way in this world.

I was always fascinated with European history and the lore of Sir Lancelot, King Arthur and the Thomas Becket, and the Canterbury Tales. The Navy allowed me to possibly fulfill my dreams. While I never made it to England, France, or the lands of knights and dragons, I spent seven months touring South America.

Following my grandparent's footsteps in reverse, sort of. When the Navy took hold of my life and moved me out of California, I found myself in North Carolina, Virginia, Ohio, and Texas. I left family and friends behind to make my mark in ways I had never considered. I believe God gave me talents, and these talents shaped me into the person I eventually became. My parents and those I encountered along the way eventually crafted my life. While I still don't believe it was written down anywhere, God, through the talents he gave me, has led me here and blessed my life far beyond anything I could have imagined.

I once heard a preacher say that only a fool would say that they would change nothing given the opportunity to live their lives over. Given a chance for a do-over, there are certain things I would change and probably do differently. I might have mended a few fences, or maybe sought out a new venture or skill. Still, I have no regrets about where my life has taken me or the life I have lived.

Every child is different. Mom always said that I was the most complacent and unlike my brothers who required constant attention, I could be placed in one spot, knowing I would not wander off. I guess you might say it was a foreshadow of just how different I would become.

2

Black Sheep Boy

Black Sheep Boy

When I was born, I did not choose to go against the grain and swim upstream. I did not set out to upset the applecart and create chaos where there was calm. It just sort of happened. Well, mostly, it just kind of happened. As I grew physically and mentally, I began to make choices I knew, deep down, would not be popular. But then, it wasn't all my fault.

I have two brothers: one older and one younger. I am in the middle in case you couldn't figure that out. My brothers were born at the Women's Hospital in Pasadena. I, too, was born in Pasadena, but not at the Women's Hospital. For whatever reason, I had to be contrary, and I arrived just before midnight on the third of July at Huntington Memorial.

When I was still an infant, my parents bought a house on Kendra Avenue in the sleepy little town of Azusa. Azusa was made famous in Warner Brothers' cartoons. Fred Quimby was an animator with Warner Brothers, and his brother lived in Azusa. His niece and I went to school together, and Sherry and I were friends. A favorite line in Fred's cartoons was,

"Who's who in Azusa's zoo?" We didn't have a zoo. We didn't even have a pet store!

Also popular on television was The Adventures of Ozzie and Harriet. One storyline had Ozzie and best friend "Thorny," played by Don DeFore, going fishing. Azusa may not have had a pet store, but it had The Azusa Hotel. This episode's filming took place at Crystal Lake, 25 miles into the mountains north of Azusa. There was no real place to stay at Crystal Lake, so the cast and crew stated at The Azusa. At that time, that was the biggest thing to happen to Azusa.

While our new house was under construction, mom, dad, and Earl examined the progress. Truthfully, I don't remember the trip at all. After all, I was the ripe old age of six months. My parents swore this story was true, but I have my doubts, though I have heard this story from my parents many times. According to their version, my grandparents told a slightly different version. Mom and dad were almost back to Pasadena when my dad turns and says to my mom, "He sure is quiet back there."

"Who?"

"Bruce!"

"He's not here. I thought you picked him up, and he's up there with you."

Dad stopped the car, and they exchanged a few nervous looks and more than a few worried words. They turned around and drove back to Virginia Avenue. There I was, eyes wide open, looking around and not making a sound. Yes, my parents left me, at six months, alone at home to fend for myself in a house that was just a wood-frame. The rafters were there, but there was no roof, and there were no walls. They had put me in a wood crate while they looked around. Excited with the progress on their home, and my make-shift cradle blended in with the surroundings, they momentarily forgot where they had put me.

Mom picked me up and made sure she had me in her arms on the way back to Pasadena.

Jack arrived about eighteen months later. We were already ensconced in our new home. Of the three, Jack was clearly the most active as a toddler.

As adults, and looking at only their headshots, it is obvious Jack was different from his brothers. Dad and Earl, and I all have relatively dark, thinning hair. Jack has a full head of thick, light brown hair. We always teased mom about Jack's hair and wondered what about the milkman's appearance.

However, standing the four of us together, especially as adults, is clear who is truly the family's black sheep. Dad and Earl look very much alike. Both wore glasses, have the same smile, and are about equal height. Jack also looks very much like dad and Earl with his full head of hair, and he, too, is six feet. Though not thin, all three are slender in build and muscular from outside work, and not working out. The little kid in the middle has the same hairline as his dad and big brother. Still, he is almost six inches shorter, stockier (a polite way of saying fatter). While there may be some resemblance in appearance, it is clear I partook of a related but slightly different gene pool. I took after my mother's side of the family. As an adult, this is even more obvious. My brothers, on the other hand, were definitely from dad's side of the gene pool.

Earl and Jack were builders and tinkerers, like my dad. Neither finished high school nor were blue-collar workers. This is not to say they were not intelligent; to the contrary. Earl followed my dad and worked for the County of Los Angeles as an Electronics Technician. Dad was an electrician and pulled the wire to provide electricity to various parts of the building. Earl used electronics to monitor air quality in Los Angeles County and held three patents for his efforts.

Jack was an entrepreneur, like his maternal grandfather. Jack was not a bricky layer but was a carpet man. Don't even think of calling him a carpet layer or carpet installer. Jack worked magic with this type of flooring. He did homes of movie and television stars who wanted carpet, but not what you would find at your nearest flooring store. Jack would inlay designs in the carpet. He used contrasting colors to create a starburst; The design would start on the floor against one wall and end at the ceiling of the wall on the opposite side of the room. Jack was not particular and did it all: residential, apartments, and commercial buildings.

My two brothers were geniuses, and I was, in many ways, in awe of what they had accomplished. I could not compete with Earl's technical skills or Jack's artistic talents. I just kind of rolled along in the background, doing my own thing. I was never quite sure what my own thing was, but I did it well!

Of the three, I was the only one that finished high school. Earl played Pony League baseball, and Jack played Little League. I wanted to try out for Little League, but dad said I didn't have what it took. Jack was the master of the visual arts.

I, more or less, mastered the theatrical, literary, and musical arms of the art world.

The one thing we all did together was enlist in the Navy. Earl was four years older than me and finished his first tour of duty when I was a high school senior. He was home and told me of the many benefits of being in the military. Before long, Early had re-enlisted and was now on a ship out of Long Beach, California, the carrier U.S.S. Oriskany. Earl was an electrical technician in the Navy, where he learned the stuff he took with civilian life.

I joined the Navy next. I became a dental technician. Theoretically, I was supposed to help a dentist fill oral cavities, take x-rays, and clean teeth. And I did this. But, unlike Earl, they stationed me in North Carolina, in an oral surgery clinic. I did a rotation in general surgery and assisted in three hernia repairs. I assisted as we reduced lower jaw and facial fractures, and I helped in bone graphs. I found myself in the morgue, the E.R., working the Teletype and being the night shift telephone PBX operator. They're the ones in old-time movies with a headset and connecting wires to a board with lots of lights.

I would eventually find my way on a ship. Actually, I was on a couple of different vessels including the destroyer tender Brice Canyon, and the frigate (also known as a destroyer leader) Norfolk, nicknamed, "The First and Finest!" Earl was on a carrier and I was on a tin-can. So much for doing the same thing.

While I was in Dental Tech School, Jack joined the Navy. No one said a word to me or gave me a heads up. When walking by a new group of recruits, I saw this tall kid with blond hair and a crooked smile. I don't remember where he was in his basic training and we only had an opportunity to do little more than acknowledge one another, but the Three Amigos, Three Musketeers, or whatever we were all in the Navy! Earl is on a carrier somewhere in the Pacific, Jack and I are together at San Diego, well, sort of. We were at the same base, but Jack was still in boot camp while I was in Dental Tech "A" school. ("A" meaning the first level of schooling. A second level would be "B" school.

My parents did not come to my graduation from Dental Tech school. My maternal grandparents, who had recently moved to Newport Beach, came to graduation and brought me home. Jack was still in boot camp for another couple of weeks. Before he finished basic training, I headed off to North Carolina. It would be more than four years before the three of us would be together again.

Upon graduation from boot camp, Jack wound up on a carrier, the Kitty Hawk. His job was to help planes land on the flat top. There are pictures and scenes in old movies of these daredevils with a paddle in each hand, guiding planes to a safe landing on this floating airstrip. That was Jack's job. One day, a plane came in a little heavy and had a difficult landing. There is a safety net along the side of the flight deck where those on deck may jump should they find themselves in danger. As the plane came in, Jack realized he was in danger and leaped into the safety net. The plane landed so hard that part of the wheel assembly came lose and landed on top of Jack. His left thigh and right tibia were both broken, and part of his leg muscles were exposed. The Navy immediately airlifted Jack to the Balboa Naval Hospital near San Diego.

Both leg muscles were exposed, and he spent a year at Balboa Naval Hospital. At any other time, Jack may have lucked out. However, this was not Jack's lucky day. The war in Viet Nam was revving up, and so instead of being medically discharged, they brought him back to active duty. Jack was told he could go anywhere he wanted, "Just say the word," they said.

"I'll go anywhere but the "Bonny Dick, the moniker the crew members gave their ship, the Bon Homme Richard" he quipped with his wry, crooked smile.

Ten days later, he's got his orders to report to . . . The Bon Homme Richard!

Because of the Viet Nam war, ships on the west coast regularly deployed to the Philippines and Viet Nam. It was not uncommon for Earl and Jack to have liberty together at one of those ports. They each had an identical tattoo, an eagle over an anchor. East coast ships were not typically deployed to Viet Nam, and since there was nothing else to do, we went to other places, like South America. I was fortunate enough to be a part of Unitas VII, a goodwill mission that took us to 22 ports around the coast of South America. I was even on Argentine television! While in Buenos Aires, the ship's band, of which I was a part, entertained between televised cock-fights. This was not prime time television. I was the accordion player and keyboardist in the band. In Argentina with a large German population, me and my accordion were the hit of the town. I was famous when I went into Buenos Aires the next day on liberty. I couldn't buy a beer or a meal!

As the three of us would laugh about it later, that we were all in the Navy, but that was the only thing in common. Earl and Jack were on the west coast, and I was on the east. They were on carriers, and I was a tin-can sailor. They went west, and I went south. They crossed the International Date Line; I crossed the equator. Even that little thing we couldn't get right! I had one more distinction over them. Our ship had an operating room. While going through the first two locks of the Panama Canal, we simulated an appendectomy with me as the patient. As I like to tell it, I went through the Panama Canal on my back.

Weeks later while traversing the Straits of Magellan, just under 400 miles from the South Pole, the simulation became reality as one of the cooks on our ship developed symptoms and had his appendix removed. I did not participate in the actual operation but was put in charge of his post-op care.

After the Navy, Earl and Jack worked a single job. I attended the University of Dayton. I worked part-time as a counter clerk/bartender at a bowling alley, an accordion teacher, and a House Technician, a fancy name for an orderly, or male attendant, at one of the smaller hospitals in Dayton, Ohio.

Earl and Jack had settled into their careers when I graduated from college. Earl would retire from the county, having worked there over 30 years. Jack was still the owner of his carpet business when he passed. Me? Well, let's just say I was different.

I graduated from U.D. with a Bachelor of Science in Education and licensed as a speech/theatre/English teacher. I taught in a half-dozen school district in two states, plus a couple more as a substitute teacher. I taught speech and theatre arts and English. I also was assigned to physical education, sixth-grade health, in-school suspension, and a host of other jobs. My last teaching job was at a juvenile correction facility where I monitored growth in reading and math, worked with special needs students, two intervention programs designed to prevent the students from heading to the adult prison system, and a host of other jobs.

Teachers also have summer jobs. So, while school was out for the summer, I found myself working as a janitor, a truck dispatcher, groundskeeper, and a projectionist at a drive-in theatre. When we were showing what the police considered an unacceptable film, it was my job to excise the offensive scenes before the movie played, and then reinstall them when it was time for the film to move on. Other jobs included working for a private detective agency specializing in insurance fraud.

I even left teaching for a while and worked as a business consultant, road-side assistance coordinator for tractor-trailer rigs needing repairs. I even managed to first store to sell or rent movies in the county. I had my own insurance agency and sold, wrote advertising copy for a local radio station and I did background checks for insurance companies.

There would be times when I would bring my wife and kids to visit. On one occasion, a friend of my parents insisted I was not their child. Mom had to intervene and assure her friend that I truly was one of the family.

One time a woman kept greeting me, "Hello, Bruce," and I had no clue who she was. Frustrated, I finally asked my mother who the mysterious woman was.

"That's your cousin, Janie. She hasn't changed a bit."

"Mom," I corrected. "It's been 30 years. She's been married, divorced, and has had three kids. Trust me. She's changed" Mom hadn't recognized that she was no longer skinny high schooler, which she was the last time I had seen her.

While Janie recognized me, her dad did not. After more than a few beers, he came up to me and introduced himself.

"Hi, I'm Luther, Thelma's brother in-law."

"I know" I said with a smile on my face. I'm Bruce. Your nephew. Embarrassed, he turned and walked away.

In many ways, we are all black sheep. Jack for the hair on his head, me for my wandering ways, and Earl for the unique challenges he had to face.

3

Earl

EARL

Earl arrived on the scene just three days before the Japanese attacked Pearl Harbor. He and his parents lived in a small, two-bedroom bungalow on Delores Avenue in Pasadena, California. Like all newborns, Earl was unique – truly unique. Earl was born with five fingers on his left hand. That is five fingers and a thumb. He essentially had two pinkies, and they amputated one a few days after birth, giving him a crooked fingerprint.

As a teenager, dad had painted a board for a project he was doing for mom. There was a left handprint on the board. Earl looked at the print and then at his hand. Then he raised his hand to dad and said, "Well, it is clear it was not me!"

Within a few months of his birth, they would draft Frank into the Army and shipped off to the South Pacific. Like so many servicemen and women, he came home a changed person. War exposes one to atrocities that cannot be imagined, and the mind has trouble comprehending. Earl discovered some of his dad's souvenirs in the attic: Japanese currency, both coin, and paper, as well as a large Rising Sun flag.

For most of the next three years, it would be just Earl and his mother. Then, just before his third birthday, Frank, his dad came home from the war, and they were a family again. There was a period of adjustment for all of the family. After three years of being a single parent, Thelma had become set in her ways in running the house. There would be times of disagreement and raised voices as the two began to work out living together again. Frank came with his own set ways as a result of three-years of warfare. Eventually, the two settled into a routine and a new rhythm of doing things evolved.

Earl had to adjust to having his dad home. Earl had fun with his mother, but he really enjoyed the roughhousing with his dad. Just as things were getting into a routine, Thelma announced she was pregnant. Soon, Earl had to contend with a new baby brother, and a big move. The family moved to a brand new home in Azusa, fourteen miles to the East.

Assimilating into family was not the only problem Fred had to face. He had some difficulty in simply adjusting to civilian life and putting the nightmares of the war behind him. The newspapers and the magazines glorified the war and the soldiers and sailors who so bravely served. No one understood the mental toll war takes upon the human mind and spirit. Mostly because Fred kept monsters of war bottled up inside, the family never understood the toll the war took on Frank.

The family settled in their new home. Fred worked for various contractors wiring new homes, then he got a job with the County of Los Angeles. We planted an Oak tree in the middle of the front yard, and three Sycamores planted in the back. The grass was growing, and life was good.

Earl was about nine or ten when it was determined that his tonsils had to come out. Today, a medical doctor removes those pesky little things, but when it was Earl's turn to have them removed, the local dentist was charged with the procedure. So, off they went to the dentist's office. The office was on the second floor of a retail section of town. I can remember standing on Azusa Avenue and looking up the long staircase. It seemed to go up forever, and it was dark at the top where there were a landing and a door with a sign reading, James Brown, DDS. Jack and I would traverse these steps in our own time, always for routine dental work. Earl was the only one destined to leave his tonsils behind.

It was not long after this that Jack came home with spots all over is body and a fever. Chicken Pox had come to visit the Stoneman family. We didn't know a lot about the disease, and Jack was kept in bed with cold compresses and aspirin for his fever. About a week after Jack recovered, I noticed strange spots on my face. It was my turn, and I was confined to bed with cold compresses and aspirin for fever. As with Jack, everyone tippy-toed around me, and everyone was attempting to be quiet.

About a week later, Earl got sick, and Jack and I figured it was Earl's turn. Something about Earl's version of the Chicken Pox was different. Whatever Earl had contracted, it wasn't Chicken Pox. No spots were appearing on his face. Jack and I both went to the doctor to confirm our infection, but Earl's infection was more serious. One Saturday, my grandparents showed up, and mom, dad, and Earl went to the doctor. What seemed like an eternity, mom and dad came home, but Earl wasn't with them.

Over hushed voices, Jack and I learned Earl had something different. Instead of Chicken Pox, we heard strange words like ambulance, hospital, and polio. Mom and dad assured our grandparents, and to some extent the two of us, that Earl would have to spend some time in the hospital, but he had a mild case of Polio and would be home soon. I am sure the adults had a better handle on this, but Jack and I were sure Earl would be home in a few days. We were unaware that polio was debilitating, crippling and sometimes, fatal.

Earl was in the child's wing of Los Angeles General, the largest hospital in the area. Mom and dad would take turns spending nights at the hospital, ensuring Earl was not alone as little as possible. The hospital had strict visiting hours. Since polio was contagious, only one parent could be in the room at a time and for only short periods of time. They spent nights in the adjacent waiting room.

A few days after they admitted Earl to LA General, our parents took Jack and me to Dr. Goodwin's office. One at a time, they took us into the examination room, dropped our pants, and crawled on the table. We were given two doses of Gamma Globulin or "GG," as the doctor called it. It was a big syringe with a red liquid inside. We were given a shot in each butt cheek. Mom held our arms, and his nurse held our legs down. The shot was not a pleasant experience. It hurt like the dickens. Truthfully, I am not sure which was worse. Seeing the big syringe with the equally large needle, or the medicine it contained. Neither Jack nor I could understand why Earl was sick or why he couldn't get this shot at get better.

"It's because Earl is sick," Mom would calmly explain. "It is too late to give him this shot. This medicine is to make sure you two will not get what Earl has." She stood there, tears rolling down her cheeks as she held us. Doctor Goodman assured her we would be alright.

"They might find it difficult sitting for the next hour or so," he said softly, with a hand on each of our shoulders. "But this should do the trick. Do watch them, and don't hesitate to call me if you have any concerns." He stood there for a few more seconds, then went through the door to his office. Then, the three of us were alone in the reception room. We stopped for an ice cream cone at Frostee Freeze on the way home. The ice cream helped, but only a little.

On Saturday, mom and dad were home early from the hospital.

"Is Earl coming home?" We eagerly asked.

"No, not right now," and they turned to my grandparents. "They are transferring Earl to Rancho Los Amigos in El Segundo. It is a special hospital just for kids with polio. We were told not to follow the ambulance. They don't go fast, but they don't stop for stop signs or signals either."

"Is Earl alright?" asked Grandma.

"He's in an iron lung," and grandma gasped, sat down, and put her head in her hands.

Every weekend for the next two years, we went to Rancho Los Amigos. Rancho Los Amigos was a converted military barrack about an hour from home. The turn off the highway took you down a long drive lined with large palms. Because of the contagious nature of the disease, only immediate family members were allowed to visit. There was a converted military guard house at the entrance where families would check in. There were four similar buildings, all with polio patients. Earl's building was the first one on the right.

There was one large room with twelve big metal tubes. There were a headrest and a mirror on top. Six tubes had the heads facing the right, and six more with heads facing the left. There was a bed opposite each tube. There were bellows below each tube and was pumping something into the tube. We later learned this was an iron lung, and the bellows were pumping air to help the sick kids breathe easier.

Mom and dad could go inside and be next to Earl; Jack and I had to stay in the hallway but could see everything. Sometimes, Earl or one of the other kids in a bed would start crying a screaming they couldn't breathe. The nurses would start up their iron lung and then struggle to get the kid into the contraption as quickly as possible. Most of the time, Jack and I could only hear what was going on as the nurse came and closed the doors. Once in a while, we would stand, scared and mesmerized, as we watched the ordeal when the nurse forgot to close the doors.

There was a large ramp leading up to the ward's entrance. Metal rails were on either side. When we were not allowed inside, Jack and I would chase each other up and down the ramp, climbing on and over them. One day, an old man with a white jacket came up and stopped us from climbing on the railings.

"You have to be careful. If you fall and get hurt, say break your arm, we can't help you."

"But" I interrupted, "This is a hospital. Hospitals take care of hurt people."

"Yes," he replied with a hint of a smile. "This isn't that kind of hospital. Unless you have an exceptional problem like these kids," pointing to the four buildings, "an ambulance will not bring you here, and your doctor will not send you here."

One afternoon, Jack and I came home from school to find mom making up the bed in the bedroom behind the living room. This third bedroom had two doors. One door led to the kitchen area, and the other to our only bathroom. Several of Earl's favorite toys and things were there, along with a brand new bed.

"Earl's coming home Saturday," she said with clear excitement in her voice. "We're putting him in this bedroom so I can keep my eye on him when I am working in the kitchen." True to her word, Earl arrived home in our car. He was lying down in the back seat, with mom and dad in the front. Dad carried Earl into the house and put him on the bed.

"Earl's still awful week from being in the hospital for so long. He has to learn how to use his muscles again, so don't expect him to play with you. He may sleep a lot, but for the time being, he will be in bed," dad explained to us. He also had a hole in his throat, a tracheotomy, which he had to cover with his finger if he wanted to talk.

A nurse came once or twice and showed mom what exercises Earl had to do.

"These exercises," the nurse began, "Were developed by a

Catholic Nun, Sister Kinney, after working with polio patients in Europe." At first, the nurse did them, and mom watched as mom was the primary one helping Earl with the exercises. The nurse came in the last two or three times; mom did the exercises with the nurse watching to make sure mom did them correctly.

Eventually, Earl got stronger and could sit up in bed, make it to a chair at his makeshift desk. He may be still sick and weak, but he was in school, and teachers made sure he had schoolwork to do so he did not get too far behind in his classes. One or two teachers regularly came to visit with Earl and check on his progress. They brought the work from all of his teachers.

Grandma Stoneman had a pet parakeet that Earl loved to talk to. When he came home, they brought him a pretty, male parakeet Earl named Petey, just like Grandma Stoneman's. This did wonders for his spirits and his progress. Earl taught Petey to talk – to say certain phrases. He would randomly say such things, "Hey, I'm a pretty bird," and "Good morning." Peaty had maybe a dozen sayings he would just blurt out. He would shake hands. Earl would stick in his finger, and Peaty would put one claw on a finger while Earl moved it up and down.

Petey was also jealous. Earl would leave the door to his cage open. Peaty would start talking, and if Earl was reading or doing schoolwork, Petey would fly over and land on the desk, or on the book, and nibble at the paper Earl was working on, or a page in the book, all the while squawking on of his favorite phrases.

We never had so much company as we did those first six months after he was home. Every relative stopped by, as well as people from our neighborhood. The doctors explained to mom and dad that Polio affected how muscles work.

"Earl has a relatively mild case of Polio" the doctor explained, "physical therapy must be done immediately if Earl is going to be able to walk normally."

A Catholic nun, Sister Kinney, developed a series of physical exercises to be done at home that would keep the leg and arm muscles active and elastic. Mom watched the physical therapist administer the exercises and eventually mom took over taking Earl through the painful routine.

Earl would eventually fully recover from Polio and even played Pony League baseball for a season or two. His tracheotomy would leave a permanent scar, and it would be a source of mild discomfort for Earl most of his life.

Earl had been home about three months when it was time to take Earl to a physical therapist. Each Saturday, mom would load us up in the car and drive to Grandma and Grandpa Deppen's. Jack and I would be given a quarter, and we'd walk the six blocks to the movies. Mom would take Earl to the physical therapist. Jack and I would get back from the movies around noon. We would eat lunch and then head home.

Jack and I were too young to fully understand what Earl was going through, but we came to cherish those Saturday mornings. The hectic confusion that was our life back then.

4

Saturday Morning Confusion

SATURDAY MORNING CONFUSION

After about three months of exercising at home, Earl had to go once a week to a physical therapist near Grandma and Grandpa Deppen's house. So, each Saturday, mom would load all three of us into the car and drive to Pasadena and Grandma Deppen's house.

Mom would take Earl to the physical therapist and gave each of us a quarter. We then walked six blocks up to the Washington Theater. For a dime, we got in to see a couple of serials. Generally, it was Gene Autry or Roy Rogers and some cartoons. Then there would be a feature film.

Another dime got us pop and popcorn, and, on the way out, we'd buy a Charms sucker. Charms were fruit-flavored, and the front part of the sucker had shapes of the fruit-flavored sucker. More importantly, we turned the sucker over and looked on the back. If we were lucky, there was a sticker with the word "Charms" on it. That meant you got a second sucker free. Jack and I would take turns buying the first sucker. No use in both buying a sucker if one had a price and we could each have one. Two suckers for the price of one.

We rarely walked straight back to Grandma's. Washington Park was two blocks from the theater, and it was a treasure trove of adventure. It was covered with bushes, and trees, and bridges. We would spend an hour each Saturday exploring the grounds. There were jungle gyms, swings, and teeter-totters. There was a stream to cross multiple times. We never left the park before our suckers were gone, and we were getting hungry.

Earl would be worn out from his therapy and asleep on the couch in the back apartment. The television would be on to a western or old movie. The western was on if Earl was there alone. The old movie was on if mom or Grandma was back there with him. That was the only television in the house.

Each summer, we would take turns spending a week with Grandma and Grandpa Deppen. Great-Grandma Haverson came out occasionally. She was from Allentown, Pennsylvania. She was small with shiny white hair. She loved to watch the soap operas while fixing the vegetables for dinner. I would sit back there with her cutting green beans or freeing peas from their pods while watching the soap operas. We talked a little, but only during commercials. She got upset if anyone should dare to interrupt her when the show was on.

Grandpa Deppen had a workshop we were not allowed in by ourselves. All kinds of things could get us into trouble. Although the door almost always unlocked, we never ventured in on our own. The threat of a specific consequence, as in a life-threatening injury, was enough to keep our curiosity in check.

Grandpa would give us a block of wood, and we would draw a design or picture on it. We would paint it, and when the paint was dry, we would give it to him. We would then retreat to the workshop where grandpa used the band saw to create a jigsaw puzzle for us.

No one was immune to the dangers of that workshop. While working on a grandma's project, he cut his left hand's ring and middle finger off. Well, almost off, they were hanging by a flap of skin when he hollered out to Grandma that phrase made famous by some astronauts years later, "We have a problem." Grandma rushed him to the hospital, where they sewed his fingers back onto his hand. It was heavily bandaged, and he had to keep the hand raised for several weeks. He never regained full use of those fingers.

We did not go in for the tools. A ban saw, a table saw, a lathe, and an assortment of hand tools. No, it was the walls that drew our attention. Or at least the top six inches of the walls. On three walls, the two side walls and the one across from the double doors were pin-ups. Girls in various stages of undress and doing 'naughty' things. One was taking a bath in a clear tub, and a couple had their nakedness hidden by strategically placed plant leaves. Everything was suggestive, and there were no body parts visible. Just suggested. It was hard for a young lad to keep his eyes off the wall. We were good-naturedly chastised by our dad and grandpa; the only real admonition was to never go in there alone.

Next to the workshop was a garage for Grandpa's work

truck. There was a five-car garage at the back of the property next to the rental cottage, but that was for cars. Grandpa's truck was a beat-up old '49 red Ford. Three-speed stick shift on the floor. The truck was never locked, but they never left keys within reach. Jack would easily become bored and left for other adventures, but I would spend hours 'driving' that truck. It might be a school bus, and I would drive the route my bus took, announcing each turn and each street from the school to home and then back to school. It was sometimes a city bus, and I drove it home, again announcing each turn and street. Mom and dad took different routes home, and I had all of them memorized. In May, it might be an Indianapolis 500 race car. If we had seen a space adventure at The Washington, it might be a spaceship. Whatever I could imagine, the truck became. Even after I got my license, I never had an opportunity to take the truck for a spin.

Grandpa only drove Buick's. He was not as pretentious as to own a Cadillac; his brother did. He also would not lower himself to own a Chevrolet. He complained a Chevy lacked the power and feel of a Buick. He would take us when we went to the store, and he would let us sit on his lap and drive the car for a few blocks. If both Jack and I were with him, we each got a turn. When I got my license, I did have the opportunity to drive the Buick and him to the store.

Mom had two accidents while driving home from Pasadena. The first was at the corner of Hudson and Mountain. Jack and I were arguing over something, and mom turned around to say something to us. She had a tendency to sometimes be a two-footed driver: one foot on the brake and one on the gas. As she turned around, her left foot left the brake while the right foot pushed slightly on the accelerator. Boom! We hit a palm tree. We sat there in silence. Jack said, "Wow!" Mom told me to go get grandpa, so I got out and ran back to Grandma's and get them. There was not much damage. We pushed the car back on the street. The accident flooded the engine, and we had to wait a few minutes before mom could start the car, and we could head home without further incident. Cars were made of metal back then, and it took more than a gentle bump into a palm tree to cause noticeable damage. We were all sworn to secrecy, and dad never knew what had happened.

The second accident happened when we were in a left-turn lane, and some man saw the light had turned green. Still, mom's car did not accelerate as rapidly as he anticipated. Boom! He hit us from behind. This time, the police had to be called, and the car had to go into the shop for some minor repairs. The car that hit us had its headlights broken, and it damaged part of the grill. We had a small dent in the trunk lid and a bent bumper. I remember the other driver saying it was mom's fault, and at the accident, she sort of agreed with him. However, the insurance company determined that mom was not at fault. The other driver's insurance company paid to have our car repaired.

Growing up, I don't remember any of us having any accidents beyond these two. Our friends would have wrecks, and a friend of Earl's, George, damaged his 53 Ford sedan. He was the 43rd car in a 43 car pile-up. It was a foggy night, and the first car stopped unexpectedly. It was a chain reaction from there. George's dad was a truck driver and was gone most of the week. When George had the accident, he called us. Dad and Earl drove to the scene of the accident and found George standing by his car, shaking his head.

"Tow truck driver said the car was most likely totaled." He said this as a matter-of-fact and never looked at Earl or dad. "I don't know what I am going to tell my dad."

Frank put a hand of George's shoulder. "We'll figure it out. Come on, let us get you home."

George's dad understood and thanked dad for being there and making sure George was not injured. After that life pretty much turned to normal.

Over the years, we always enjoyed riding to the Deppen's and the Stoneman's. Earl had his coveted seat behind the driver. Jack and I would argue over who sat in the middle, and who had the window seat. I sort of liked the middle seat because the other two were looking out the window, I was pretending to drive. Although mom or dad did most of the driving, I did get to drive once in a while.

In all of those weekend trips, whether we were going there, or they were coming to our house, I don't recall another auto mishap. Not even when I had an opportunity or two to do the driving.

Earl was the serious one. He seemed to have something on his mind almost all of the time. Jack was the prankster. If there was some mischief to be found, Jack found it. I was known as the entertainer.

5

The Squeezebox

THE SQUEEZEBOX

Danny and the Juniors had a big hit called "At the Hop." The three of us did lip-synch of the song with Earl taking the lead, and we performed it for our parents. It was a lot of fun, but it was the only number that all three of us liked that we could do as a group.

Earl was into anything rock-and-roll loved Elvis. Jack was also into rock-and-roll, and his favorite was Ricky Nelson. I was the strange one and loved the old songs. For Christmas, I got a Ricky Nelson album, and Jack got one by Bobby Darin. The Ricky Nelson had a couple of songs he performed on his parent's television show. The Darin had featured one hit song; the rest were re-workings of old songs, and I loved it. Who knows, maybe the tags got mixed up, and we got each other's gift. Either way, Jack and I switched albums, and we could not be happier.

I would spend time in the bedroom listening to music. Jack would jump around playing his air guitar and swiveling his hips a la Elvis. Jack knew the words to all the pop songs currently on the radio. Me? I particularly enjoyed Jerry Lee

Lewis and Fats Domino because they were piano players. I'd sit and play the piano-bed for hours.

One evening, a gentleman – a salesman – came to the door with a big box. Mom and dad had me go in and listen to him. He opened his box, and there was this bright, shiny black and white Enrico Roselli piano accordion. It had a ton of buttons on the left side. There were two switches on the left side and three on the right. I learned the black buttons on the left provided the chords, and the right hand, on the piano keyboard, plays the melody. The switches would affect how the air went over the reeds and change the accordion's sound.

The salesman had a second, smaller box, and there was a miniature version of his accordion. It had only twelve buttons on the left and a smaller keyboard on the right. There were no switches to change the sound. He fitted the accordion to my body and helped me make some music or noise depending upon your perspective. When he left, I was the proud owner of a new accordion. Actually, we rented the accordion. If I progressed to a larger accordion, what we paid in rent for the smaller version would apply to the larger model, which we would own.

A week or two later, a little old lady in a small blue and white car pulled into the driveway. She got out, and when mom answered her knock, she introduced herself as Ms. Wentworth, the accordion teacher. She was sweet and patient and gave me some exercises for me to practice on the accordion. She told me I was a natural. What else was she going to say, that I am horrible? Either way, before long, she had me playing real tunes on the accordion.

Grandma and Grandpa Stoneman's favorite television show was "The Lawrence Welk Show." He, and his sidekick, Myron Floren, played accordions. Welk would introduce the songs and start directing his orchestra, and Myron was a featured accordion player in his orchestra. Every once in a while, the two would play a duet on matching accordions. I don't know if it was because we could not afford a piano or if grandma and grandpa had a hand in convincing my parents to give the accordion a try. Either way, I was now an accordionist.

Jack and I spent the time after my lesson while mom was paying for my day's lesson, going over Mrs. Wentworth's car. It was not our first foreign car as my godfather would drive an MG Roadster when he would visit. But his was a small, compact sedan imported by American Motors called a Metropolitan. I can't really place my finger on why we were so intrigued by it, but we were. One week, the lesson was on a Saturday, and knowing that the two of us were interested in her car, she took us for a ride around the block. That was the highlight of our week.

It wasn't long before there was another discussion, and I was the proud owner of a full-sized 120 bass accordion. It had three treble switches. A treble switch moved the sound up a notch, and a tenor switch moved the sound down a notch. The master put the two together.

With the larger accordion came more challenging music. Some of the music had melody played with the buttons. The key was knowing where the middle C button was. The accordion bass buttons were all the same, so dad got out a sharp knife and marked the three landmark buttons. There was middle C, the E button on top, and the A-flat button on the bottom. Rather than guessing and trying out the buttons until I found the right one, my fingers could easily find them. Unlike the instrument's piano side, the buttons were not visible, and the markings made playing much more comfortable.

Each week, I was given a new song to learn. Generally classical in nature. It might be a song such as Fur Elise by Beethoven, a Sousa march, or a polka such as Beer Barrel Polka or The Clarinet polka. I do not know whether it was a requirement or an expectation. Still, I would have music assigned from the previous lesson memorized when she came the following week. It got to the point that before I went to bed that night, I would have the day's lesson mostly, if not wholly memorized.

Along with the larger accordion came mandatory public performances. Each month, we would go to the Odd Fellows Lodge in Baldwin Park for a recital. We needed to bring along our accordion and our music. They provided music stands. Part of the music lesson was an accordion band piece. When we got together, the director would identify which part of the music each of us would play. Most of the students were assigned just one section, and that was decided during the lesson. A couple of us were asked to practice both parts so we could be put where needed.

After the accordion band played, she required us to play a solo. It could be any of the songs taught that month, and it did not have to be memorized. My lessons were on Thursday evening, and the recitals were on Saturday. I always chose the most recent assignment and memorized the piece.

Ricky and Eddie were brothers living behind our house. Ricky played the trumpet, and Eddie played the trombone. We were all in the junior high band. However, since the accordion was not a band instrument, I attempted to play the drums. The three of us formed a combo. Our junior high had a talent show each year we were in junior high, and we would play a pop song. I would buy the sheet music and was the leader. I purchased the piece and verbally arranged the song, telling each where their solo came in. I would introduce the song and get us started.

I was in the Boy Scouts. Each year, the scouts in the area would get together at the National Guard Armory and demonstrate various scouting skills. There was always entertainment, and they asked me to perform twice. I would play two or three songs, including songs part of my music lesson, and part was from sheet music of popular songs that I had purchased. I always memorized my music.

Mom could not read music but could play by ear. When I would practice, she would come in, have me work the bellows, and play a song she had just heard on the radio. She tried to teach me but playing by ear is something you either have a talent for or don't. I didn't. It was OK because I could read music.

Music and performing would be a big part of my life. Starting in elementary school with a shadow play and the elementary choir. I was even a soloist. In junior high and high school, I attempted to play the drums. In college, I met Danny Scribbs from New Orleans and we formed a Zydeco band.

This continued into high school. I was in the French Club, and the French teacher would take operas, and we would perform highly edited versions, karaoke-style. We would put them on for the public.

I was in two of these operas: "Carmen," and "Orphee aux Enfers," or "Orpheus in Hell." "Carmen" remains one of my favorite operas, with "The Toreador Song" being the most recognizable. The Orpheus piece featured the original can-can music, and it was during this play, I got my first kiss. Not just my first stage kiss, but my first kiss period. Jenny kept saying to me, "Now, don't you laugh." I had an embarrassed smile from ear to ear during rehearsals. Still, I managed to get through both performances without laughing as she planted a kiss on my lips!

My first high school had a school carnival and clubs and activities put on demonstrations, sold trinkets, or performed something. My French grades frustrated my teacher to no end because I had no trouble reading or speaking French. I had low grades, even failing grades because I did not take homework seriously. For the carnival, we performed an Aesop fable of the "Lion and the Mouse" entirely in French. David Jolie, president of the club, said to me as we were building the set, "I don't know why you're working on this. You will never get a part in the play. Your French is so horrible, you can't even pass the class."

He had thrown the gauntlet down.

I helped build the set, and then it came for auditions.

David and I both auditioned for the lead, the part of the lion. David's grades in class were much better than mine, which did not take much, but he had difficulty memorizing lines. He would skip a line, turn the line around, or forget the line altogether. On the other hand, I had not only learned my part but the entire play. Much to David's chagrin, I won the part. David got mad. He refused a lesser role, and because he was no longer the lead and the most crucial person in the play, he did not even show up for the performance. We put it on three or four times during the carnival, and I enjoyed it thoroughly.

During my senior year, my parents moved, and I had to switch high schools. When it came for our open house, my senior English class was to perform scenes from Hamlet. New to the school, I did not know many people. I also assumed most teachers did not know me. However, impressed with my reading and class participation, Dr. Ewing, my English teacher, was. He talked me into trying out for the role of Hamlet. Three brief scenes were to be performed, including the famous "To be or not to be" soliloquy. I agreed, and much to my surprise, I won the part. We performed the scenes multiple times that night.

In the meantime, the accordion had moved to be just a hobby, and I played only at home. I became good friends with the manager of the local music store, Shining Strings Studios, and bought sheet music for the popular tunes of the day. He introduced me to Tom, a saxophone player. He tried to teach me the saxophone, and I helped him with the accordion. But school came first, and graduation was soon upon us.

The accordion and theatre would become an integral part

of my adult life. I would spend a quarter-century as choir director for my church. The choir would take time off during the summer, and at least one Sunday, I would be up there playing my heart out, arranging the music on the fly.

As a theatre arts teacher, I would direct more than fifty plays, including musicals, operas, dramatic and comedic plays. Most of my schools did not have a choir, so I would bring my squeezebox to school to both entertain and help the students learn the music. This was particularly useful when I was directing a play and the actors had to sing a song. The playwright wrote the words, but no music was provided. I wrote the music and the accordion taught them the melody.

Music and theatre would shape me into the man I would become and through the years, I would come to appreciate the creativity of the soul. Earl and I each had our creative moments. However, we could not hold a candle to Jack!

6

The Fort, The Cart and Other Adventures

THE FORT, THE CART AND OTHER ADVENTURES

In our neighborhood, the lots were large. As Azusa grew, people were looking for places to live, and current residents were looking for ways to cash in on the size of their lots. It was not uncommon for people to supplement their income by building duplexes in the backyard. The yards were deep enough to provide for a duplex with each side having a single-car garage, and everyone had their own green space.

We divided Our back yard in half, separated by a chain-link fence. We landscaped the front half and manicured it. Three sycamore trees lined the south fence. One of these hit the septic tank and grew to more than thirty feet tall. Jack and I would climb this tree, and about three quarters up, it was possible to see the entire city essentially. We could spot the bowling alley on highway 66, over five miles away. It was an awesome sight. At the end of the 50s, we would convert the garage into a workspace, and eventually, my bedroom.

The far back was a different story. Whatever grass was back

there had grown on its own. We rarely watered it. It was the part of the yard designated as the play area. There was no grass, flowers, or anything else to tear up. We did have a garden behind the incinerator one year. We grew corn, tomatoes. Our neighbor, Fred, raised chickens and rabbits. We would sometimes trade fresh vegetables from our garden for a freshly killed chicken or rabbit.

One summer, dad got a two-car garage for a workshop. The house also got new aluminum siding. The front had a faux rock on the bottom half and siding on the upper half. It was a significant improvement in the house's look.

As part of the garage addition, we added a massive patio. It stretched from the house to the new garage, about 20 feet. The patio was about half as long as well. Mom and dad liked to throw parties, and this was the perfect spot! We could have all the relatives over for a cookout and still have enough green space for the kids to play.

We had a clothesline with two large T-poles supporting the lines. It was located right behind the old garage. When we built the new garage, it was moved to behind the new garage. Jack and I used to use the original clothesline as a makeshift ladder. We would climb the T-post close to the house and then climb onto the roof. Moving down the line, and feet dangling off the roof, we'd play daredevil and see how far away from the house we could launch ourselves. Each of us would practice on our own, and Jack was the hands-down winner. One day, Jack was on the roof when mom came home from work. She spotted his head over the roofline and got around back just in time to hear Jack let out a war hoop and see him take a standing leap.

"That's enough, she said," with a reddened face. "If I catch you, or Bruce, ever on the roof and jumping, I am going to tell your dad." She stood there with her hands on her hips for a few minutes then added, with a hard to hide smile, "We can't afford no broken bones right now."

The far back was our designated area, and dad and Earl built and erected our own basketball backstop. We would play two-on-two for hours on Saturday mornings. My dad and Grandpa Deppen also built a two-seat merry-go-round. Two would sit on a cross board, such as you would find on a teeter-totter, only this one stayed level to the ground. There was a handle, and a third person would spin you. Being older and more muscular, Earl could get Jack and me going at a pretty good clip. No matter how hard either of us tried, we could never match Earl's speed.

Grandpa Deppen was a mason: a bricklayer. When we first moved in, it was expected people would burn the paper as curbside pickup of trash had not yet come to our neighborhood. Each night, we would take the papers and cans out to the incinerator and set the contents ablaze. It resembled a grey chimney with a metal door on the front incline. There was a metal grate inside where the trash was placed. At the end of the week, and after the ashes cooled, we would dig out the tin-cans, which we would take to a recycling place. Since we had to make our own forms of entertainment, we included the incinerator in our fantasies. It became rockets, forts, and a host of other things. At Christmas, our personal chimney as we pretended to be Santa Claus and slide down the fireplace chimney.

Two major problems with this toy. First, the ashes on top may have been cool. However, there were often pockets of hot ashes, and our shoes and jeans would get scorched from the heat. They wouldn't catch fire, just turn everything a bit brownish. The other problem, it was a dirty place to play – which made it even more exciting. It also meant a bath before we could eat dinner was in the cards.

They built Our neighborhood in a prehistoric riverbed, and you could barely put a shovel in the ground without hitting a rock. So, my parents, their parents, and probably their siblings would come out a move wheelbarrow after wheelbarrow full of rocks to the edge of the property. Our rock pile would eventually be fifty feet wide, about two feet tall, and four feet deep. It was a mound of rocks of all sizes, and we would have mock battles with one side on the far side of the pile protecting the neighbor's fence from an enemy, which had to approach through an open field.

It was also a source of primitive weaponry. Everyone seemed to have the same pile, and it ran probably eight houses up from the highway. Rock fights were commonplace. Some of these fights were part of a game. Other times, Jack and I would get into a fight and wind up at the rock pile. We'd try to get close enough to be a target but far enough away to avoid serious injury. When we'd get into a fight, and what brothers didn't fight, one of us, usually Jack, would be at our pile and the other, usually me, about fifty feet down the alley.

We would then hurl insults at each other, each followed by a stone.

We would get in trouble for having a rock fight, and mom would protest that it was too easy to poke an eye out with a rock. The truth was, we were in little danger as even if we got hit, the rock rarely bruised us, let alone cut skin. We were far enough away that when we would get hit, it was in the belly or the legs, and an occasional rock hit our chest. Never, ever, did anyone get hit anywhere near the neck and head. In all the years of rock fights, not one required a band-aid, let alone a hospital trip for a lost eye.

One year, I got a prop-rod for Christmas. This was a race car with an engine and propeller on the back, which proved to be a painful if you didn't get your fingers out of the way quickly enough. You'd put 'gasoline' in the engine; it came with its own special fuel and pump. I would fill the engine with the special fuel. It smelled a lot like lighter fluid, prime the engine and then flip the propeller to get the engine started. The propeller propelled the car down the road. To have more control and less danger, we attached some lines to one side of the car, which was then attached to a pole by a machine washer. Once the engine got started, the car would go around and around until it ran out of gas. The pit crew was always on duty. If the string broke, the car would go flying, and the propeller would break. We would replace both the string and the propeller and be back in business in a few minutes.

Jack, however, had his sights on bigger and better cars. We started out building scooters by cannibalizing our old metal roller skates, and we were in business. Later, under his design and guidance, we built a series of pushcarts. Jack commandeered axles and wheels from our wagons, scrap lumber our dad kept behind the garage, and voila, a pushcart. There was a makeshift seat, and one end of a piece of rope was fastened to each side of the axle. Like riding a sled in the snow, you pulled on the right side of the rope to go right and the left to go left. voila

We started off pushing on the seatback, but that was gruesome and hard on the back. We found it was much easier and less painful to push in the driver's shoulders. Jack devised a slot in the back of the seat where a pole, compliments of an unused closet, and it was easier to push with the pole, and it attained more speed.

At the same time, the term go-cart snuck into our vocabulary. These were a single seat cart powered by a Briggs & Stratton lawnmower engine. There were two companies in town making these new toys, and Jack called each and got catalogs sent to the house. We ogled over which model we would get. Although relatively inexpensive, the $125 price tag pretty much kept it out of our reach.

But Jack had an idea, and the school bus stop was at the drive of a junkyard. Jack priced and found he could get a car's steering wheel for a couple of dollars. As usual, he did not have the money, so it came out of my copper-colored, telephone-shaped bank. He bought a white one and brought it home. He immediately began designing a new cart, one with a steering wheel. Dad drilled a hole in the closet rod's center, and Jack went about building the car.

The finished product was a sight to behold. You put your

feet on a running board and only used them for a brake. You could actually steer with the steering wheel. As we learned, it was important how you wound the rope around the rod and attached the ends to the front axle. With Jack at the helm, I pushed him down the street. He turned the steering wheel to the right, and the car gently turned left and hit our neighbor's left rear tire. That's when we realized we wound the rope the wrong way.

Bradley was the neighborhood bully and was always giving everyone a hard time. He watched from his front porch and saw what he believed to be a fun ride. Jack was always crashing into something, so Bradley naturally assumed the turn into the car was intentional. Although we attempted to dissuade him from riding, we could not pass up the chance to embarrass him simultaneously. So, after some half-hearted protests, we set the car up for Bradley's turn. Both Jack and I pushed the car for extra speed, and whereas Jack was going up a slight incline, Bradley was going down a slight decline, meaning his speed would be even faster.

Moving quickly down the street, he saw a car turn the corner and coming in his direction. He was at his driveway and turned to the right, expecting a smooth landing. Instead, he actually swerved into the car's path, hit the curb hard, and came to an abrupt stop.

Bradley was the only one on the street to curse regularly. Any curing on our part reported to or heard by mom would mean we would have our mouths washed out with Ivory soap. It was a popular brand as it floated in the water, but it did not taste pleasant. When Bradley got up from his ride, he had more than a few choice words for Jack and me, and we learned a couple of new curse words. He threatened to beat us up if we came his way again anytime soon, but we knew it was hot air coming from a sore chest. The cart had no seat belt, and while the cart came to an abrupt stop, Bradley didn't until his chest met the steering wheel.

Jack restrung the rope, and it corrected the steering problem. Except for Bradley, who never wanted to ride that cart again, all the neighborhood kids had fun riding it until it hit one too many curbs and the front axle split. Which was fine with us. We were getting tired of pushing everybody, and Jack's mind was heading in another direction.

Although Southern California days could be hot, the evenings benefited from a coastal breeze and cooled down in the evening. We would occasionally plan asleep out in the backyard. Dennis lived catty-corner to our house and invited Jack and me for a sleepout at his house. Dennis went all out and pitched a tent, and we built a small fire. We roasted hot dogs and marshmallows. It was a night that we truly roughed it. His parents ran an extension cord out to the tent. As we settled down for the night, we watched television on a small, portable television.

Jack was a bit more rustic, and each summer for three or four years, we established a residence in the backyard. The first year, it was primarily tape and cardboard. It lasted a few nights and was a noble experiment. However, after seeing what Jack had created out of cardboard, dad would bring scrap lumber from various jobs home. Jack and I would put together a wooden fort. Sometimes, there would be windows and a door. Sometimes, there would be only a door, but the last fort not only had no door, it only peepholes for windows.

Periscopes were a favorite toy of the day. Most were purchased at the local five and dime and were constructed out of cardboard with aluminum foil for refractors. For one fort, Jack built a periscope out of wood and mirrors from mom's makeup compacts. We cut a hole in the ceiling and could raise up the periscope and observe any intruders.

Sometimes, Jack and I would spend the night alone in the fort, and other times, we would invite a friend or two to join us. The last fort was truly designed exclusively for Jack and me, and a select few friends. Not that we put a lock on the door, as we had on previous forts, as there was no door. In and out was by a hole dug in one corner of the fort. To say that Jack and I were skinny would be putting it mildly. So, only us string-beans could enter the fort. Our link to the outside was strictly by periscope. We could see intruders long before they saw the tip of the periscope. If it was someone we didn't want in the fort, we just sat quietly in the fort until they left, confirmed by a periscope sighting. The following year, Jack started playing Little League, which ended the Jack Stoneman Fort Construction Company.

Because homes had no air conditioning, our entire family would lie out sleeping bags, pillows, and blankets and spend the night under the stars. Just as when Jack and I were in the fort, I was the last to fall asleep. I was fascinated with the night sky and sounds. Sometimes, I would still be awake, faking sleep as my parents got up, went in the house to prepare the family breakfast.

Those were some of the best summer nights–ever! And as we all know, as summer ends, school begins.

7

Rhoades Avenue Elementary

RHOADES AVENUE ELEMENTARY

When most school districts need a new school, they build the school and then populate it. It may take a year or so to build the school, but then it is done, and that is that. Rhoades Avenue was unique. It took four years to build, and it was occupancy grew throughout the construction.

They built the administrative wing, cafeteria, and gymnasium first, and the first wing of classrooms housing first and second graders. I started at Rhoades Avenue in the first grade. As we completed each school year, they added a new wing. Thus, as I moved into second grade, the third and fourth-grade wing was completed. When I was in third grade, the fifth and sixth-grade wing was completed. When I moved into fifth grade, they opened two kindergarten classrooms, and the school was complete.

Azusa moved from an agricultural community, raising vegetables and growing citrus fruits to becoming a mixture of a bedroom community and a small industrial town. Any new construction almost always included clearing away abandoned fruit trees. They built Rhoades Elementary School in an abandoned orchard purchased by the district. The construction included clearing away more of the orchard for the next phase of the school. Because the district-owned the orchard, any oranges growing on the trees were fair game. At lunch or recess, there were always groups venturing into the remaining orange trees' first rows and helped ourselves to free oranges. Although most were picked for eating, boys will be boys, and some of the oranges, especially those beyond fit for human consumption, became projectiles.

We lived within a half-mile of the school, so bus transportation was out of the question. At that time, most mothers did not work outside of the house, and they would take turns walking neighborhood kids to school. When I was in second grade, we had an unusually wet fall, and the area was prone to flooding. The San Gabriel's kept the moisture in the valley. Rain would start at the mountain tops and move southwest into Azusa and surrounding areas. Never a tall kid, I remember mom helping us cross one of the busier streets that had flooded. The rain had come during the day, and when she came to walk us home, we had some difficulty crossing the street with the rushing water. It was just a nuisance for mom, but it was waist-deep and a major obstacle for a short, skinny second-grader. Like many Southern California communities, Azusa would eventually build concrete riverbeds to capture the water and move it through town without flooding the entire city. When I was in second grade, they were still on the drawing board and would be years before becoming a reality.

When I was in third grade, Earl and his best friend, Jerry,

were in junior high. Every once in a while, mom would tell Earl that he and Jerry were to walk me to school. This was not something they were particularly fond of doing. One day they had a little fun. Instead of walking on Rhoades Avenue to the front of the school, they went the back way along Marvin Street. Between Marvin and the school was the orange orchard that was being cleared a little more each year as the school was being built. Earl and Jerry walked me into the orchard and left me with instructions to continue walking to the school. Having done what they believed was their duty, they turned and high-tailed it out of the orchard and on their way to their school. They figured I would get to school a little late, but I would arrive unharmed.

Wrong!

From my vantage point, all I could see were trees and oranges. There was not a lot of noise or traffic at that time. Although both Marvin and Rhoades Avenue would become major thoroughfares, they were rarely traveled when I was in second grade. I could not walk toward and discernable sound. I spent the morning in tears and calling for help; essentially, I was walking in circles. It wasn't until lunch when the entire school was outside, and some of those brave souls wanting a free orange heard my wailing.

I heard one of the kids go and bring a teacher back to the edge of the orchard.

"There's someone crying in there," one told the teacher.

"Are you sure?" she asked in a quizzical tone.

"Just listen."

A few seconds later, Mrs. Thurman, my teacher, found me sitting against a tree.

"What are you doing in here? Why didn't you come to school?"

"I got lost," is about all I could get out.

Once inside the classroom, and I had settled down, I explained to Mrs. Thurman how Earl and Jerry had walked me to school. How they left me in the orchard as they went on to their school.

When I got home, mom was waiting for me. The school had apparently called and explained what had happened. She cornered Earl when he got home from school.

"I took him to school like you said," he mumbled. "We went up Marvin because Jerry and I were going to be late for school ourselves. We walked Bruce more than half-way through the orchard and told him to keep walking in the same direction, and he would be on the playground. It's not our fault he didn't keep walking."

Dad was working out of town for the week and never learned of the incident. The one major consequence was fine with Earl and Jerry. They never had to walk me to school again.

The following year, I had Mrs. Stearns for third grade. She was a kind, grandmotherly type. We held her husband in awe by most of us because he was a guard at Paramount Movie Studios. He would regale us with stories of movie stars that he knew and various movie sets he had been on.

Alfred Hitchcock made a movie, Dial M. For Murder, which was based on a stage play. Mrs. Stearns had a copy of the stage play and decided we would perform the play as a "shadow play." We strung up sheets across the front of the room with lights clipped to the chalkboard. The story was read, and we acted out the play with the audience seeing only shadows.

We had two casts. I was the murderer in one cast, and it was my job to turn on and off the lights as needed when the other cast performed. It was the very first of many plays with which I would be involved over the years.

I was always known as the helpful one – at home and at school. I have always had a hard time saying “no” when asked to help or do a favor.

For example, in fourth grade, trying to be helpful, I almost died. At least, that what our family doctor told me. The windows at Rhoades did not go up and down. The bottom window flipped open. Cathy, a classmate, tried to close the window at the end of the school day and could not get it closed. I went out the back door and put two hands on the window and pushed. The window closed forcefully, and unfortunately, I had only one hand on the window frame. The left hand was on the window itself, and as the window stopped, my hand did not. My left hand went through the window and tore my left wrist open.

Blood gushed everywhere. Holding my left arm, I ran crying and screaming down the walkway to the office. A couple of teachers intercepted me, saw what was wrong, and got me into the nurse's office. Our nurse serviced two different campuses and had just left for the other campus. The assistant principal grabbed cotton balls and placed in over the wound while the secretary called my mother.

My arm was wrapped in blood-soaked gauze when we arrived at Doctor Goodin's office. I immediately went in and laid down on the examination table. I don't like needles and turned away when I got two or three shots to deaden the arm. I then watched in amazement as he cleaned the wound. "They should never have used cotton," he muttered as he used tweezers to remove strands of bloody cotton. It took thirteen stitches. I was given a clean bandage and a sling to keep my arm both slightly elevated and immobilized.

"You are one lucky young man," Doctor Goodin began. "You almost cut an artery in your arm. Cut that, and you could have bled to death before you could get here." I do not know if he was trying to scare me, which he did, or if he was just trying to get me to be more careful. He didn't have to worry about that. I could never again help close windows at school!

The first two or three bandage changes were still bloody. But eventually, the bleeding stopped. They removed the stitches, and I finished my treatment with a simple gauze wrap the mom could change at home.

For more than a year, I could follow my blood trail from the classroom to the office. A put a new school rule in place, and it allowed no students to open or close the windows. That became a teacher-only duty. For about a week, I was a celebrity on campus and even got a couple of handmade cards. Eventually, everything subsided, and the only reminder of my incident was the fading blood splatters on the ground.

There is a circular scar on my left arm that serves as a reminder of what happened on that fateful day. Looking back, I know I am lucky to have just that one scar. Especially considering we were now playing around fast-moving freight trains.

8

San Gabriel 1959

SAN GABRIEL 1959

One of the most potent memory triggers is music. When I was a youngster, I had the mumps- twice. I was home, in bed with the mumps. It was 10:30 in the morning at the Lloyd Price song, "Stagger Lee," which had just played on the radio. The announcer on the radio broke in.

"We have just learned an airplane crash has killed rock-and-roll giants Buddy Holly, The Big Bopper, and Ritchie Valens." Or, at least, words to that effect. That was 1958, and I cannot hear the song "Stagger Lee" without thinking of that tragic day immortalized in the song, "American Pie." Likewise, I can't talk or think about that day without hearing "Stagger Lee" that had just played when I learned of the crash.

Many engaged couples have "our song," the song they will dance to when it comes to their first dance as husband and wife. Every time they hear that song, they cannot help, but their mind will recall that momentous occasion.

"Texas 1947" tells of a town gathering at the train station to witness the first diesel-fueled train rolling through town. The song is from the perspective of a young boy who managed to put a nickel on the track before the train came through, and he retrieved it after I had smashed it.

The 40s and 50s were a much simpler time, and we did things that parents and society would not allow in the decades that followed. The song immediately took me to the 50s in San Gabriel, California. My mom would drag us three boys along as she went to visit her sister, Darleen. Darleen has four kids, two boys and two girls. The middle two were the same age as Jack and me. Near to their house was a busy rail line with freight trains traveling through regularly, going both ways.

Physics fascinated us; only we were too young to appreciate what we were witnessing. A train would come through, and we would put pebbles on the track. The train's weight would pulverize the stone and send puffs of dust in all directions as it crushed the rock between the wheels and the track. Our parents warned us against this thrill, saying we could cause the train to come off the track.

One day, Jack, the most adventurous of us all, put a penny on the track. None of us was sure what would happen, and we hid behind our usual little wall, part of a drainage system, as the train raced past. When the drain was safely down the track, Jack retrieved his penny; only it was not a penny anymore.

When Jack put the penny on the track, it was dirty bronze, but it was bright, shiny, and paper-thin when he retrieved it. The train pressed it into an oval shape. There was nothing but the color to remind anyone that it was once a penny.

Over time, we had put pennies, nickels, dimes, and quarters on the track for trains to smash and polish. Our parents put the kibosh on the practice. Not so much as a safety issue, but a costly one. A penny would buy you a jaw-breaker or a ball of bubble gum. A nickel could get you a candy bar or a small coke – we all carbonated beverages "coke" when I was a boy. A quarter got you into a movie, a sucker, popcorn, and maybe a penny or two left over.

Today, kids do not have the opportunity to experience the raw energy up close and in person. Oh, you can still flatten a penny, but it will cost you an additional four bits. Museums, novelty shops, and airports have machines in which you put two quarters and a penny in a slot. You push the coins in, crank a handle, and out comes a shiny, copper oval disk embossed with some message or image. They make excellent souvenirs, and some people collect them.

Be it in Texas, 1947 or California, 1946 or elsewhere where there were kids, pebbles, coins, and a railroad track, and things got smashed. It was a lot more fun to see physics in action than reading about it in a boring textbook.

One Christmas, Earl, got his first HO gauge train set. It was a lot fancier than the large scale, metal track that Jack and I had. But then, Christmas was always a magical time.

9

The Three Days of Christmas

THE THREE DAYS OF CHRISTMAS

Christmas is always a special time, and we celebrated Christmas three times each year. Sometimes, we would spread it over three days; other times, we condensed it to two. Regardless of whether it was two days or three days, we always had three distinct celebrations. The first one was always at Grandma and Grandpa Deppen's. The second was always at home, and the third was always at Grandma and Grandpa Stoneman's. The first was the most festive, the second was the most fun, and the final one was the most formal and sedate.

Christmas at the Deppen's was one large party. There were aunts, uncles, and cousins galore. The house itself was a large Craftsman-Style house with a large living room and formal dining room combined. Spread over the formal, massive dining room table was a large ham with loaves of bread and vegetables, all fresh and homemade. There was a fireplace and a large Christmas tree in the corner to the right of the fireplace. There was a large kitchen with another large, informal dining area just off to the kitchen's left. The women were in the informal dining area with the kids in the back apartment. The men were on the large patio at the back of the house.

When the sun went down, grandpa started a fire in the fireplace, and we turned tree lights on. The tree was always fresh, and pine aroma filled the space. Festively wrapped packages were under the tree and constantly under the watchful eye of the children.

In the early evening, everyone would gather in the dining-living rooms and sing Christmas carols. Around seven, there was a knock at the front door, and in came Santa Claus, fully decked out in red with a snow-white, flowing beard. He had a bag of presents, and after talking with each of the cousins, he would pull his bag open and distribute presents to all the cousins. All the presents were the same, and yet unique at the same time. This year, everyone got a book.

Jamie, a cousin living halfway between our grandparents and us, got a book she had already read. I opened mine, and while I had not already read the book, it was a title I already had. We agreed to swap books, and this upset Jack to no end.

"That present was from Santa. You can't switch them!"

He was almost in tears and would not listen to our explanation. Our parents came over and explained what we had done. Everyone smiled, and mom took Jack aside to console him.

After all the presents were distributed, grandma took Santa by the arm. Everyone began singing, "I Saw Mama Kissing Santa Claus." When the song ended, she planted a sweet kiss on his cheek. He wished us all a Merry Christmas and went out the door.

Mom and her sisters took the lead and began distributing presents to everyone. Whereas only the cousins got presents from Santa, everyone had at least one present under the tree. Soon, the whole area was littered with paper, ribbon, and tags. Dad brought in a shiny trash can, and we stuffed all of the trash into the can, to the point it could not hold another scrap.

Around nine, the party broke up, and we all headed to our houses. Once home, mom ushered us to bed with promises that Santa would soon be there. We never discussed it openly, but each wondered silently how Santa was going to get into the house since we didn't have a fireplace.

"Don't fret so much," mom would say. "He's Santa. Trust me, he will get in without a problem."

Jack and I shared a bedroom, and each struggled to stay awake until midnight to hear just how Santa got into our house. We never made it. After all, we surmised, he wouldn't come if we were awake.

Our Christmas tree was in the southeast corner of the living room. Most of the time, we had a real tree, and the aroma from the tree filled the air. Unfortunately, I was allergic to most real trees and constantly sneezed when in the living room. In fact, my nickname was 'Sneezy' because I had so many allergies and was constantly sneezing.

One year, we set aside the whole allergy problem when we had a shiny aluminum tree. It was too dangerous to put lights on the tree, so there was a light with a tricolor wheel the rotated when on. The tree went from blue to red to yellow and back to blue again.

One year, we bought a tree early, and by the time Christmas Eve came, it was just about dead. Coming home from the Deppen's, we found a tree lot closed with one or two scrawny trees remaining. We stopped and took one. Before we went to bed on Christmas Eve, we took down one tree and put up and decorated a new tree.

There is a movie where a little boy wants a BB gun but is told he can't have one because, as he is repeatedly told by his parents, "You'll shoot your eye out." He eventually gets one, and sure enough, he shoots himself in the eye. He wore glasses, and the BB shattered the eyeglass but did not hurt his eye.

I was not into guns, but I was into chemistry. The number one wishes every year was a chemistry set. I don't know if my parents thought I'd make a bomb or catch the house on fire, but I never got the chemistry set. One year I got a microscope. The next year, a telescope, I was afraid to hear the rationale, so I never did ask why Santa never brought me my chemistry set.

One year, one of the hottest toys was a hand-held metal loop called a Wheely. A red wheel with two shiny metal spokes that were magnets and the wrist's moving made the wheel move up and down the wires.

Mom's best friend worked for a toy company, but not the one that made the magnetic wheel toy. They did make their own non-magnetic version of the toy which Santa gave to me. The toy with the little red wheel was about a foot long. I found a box about a yard long with my name on it. I eagerly tore the paper off the present and stared at the present.

"Oh, boy! Just what I wanted!" I lied. I had seen nothing

like it before. It was a green ladder-like contraption with yellow cups at one end and just above the handle. Three ping pong balls bounced on the floor. I looked dumbfounded at my parents for guidance.

"What is it?" is about all I could say.

"It's a Ladder-Ball," mom said with enthusiasm. "You put a ball on one side and tile the handle down. When it goes through the yellow tube at the end, you turn the ladder over and lift it up. The ball comes down and goes through the yellow tube, you turn your hand back, and the ball goes down the ladder again." She is showing this with considerable adeptness while she is explaining how to do it. It took me most of the day to master it well enough, so the ball did not fall off as I failed to turn and lift the ladder as quickly as needed.

Jack ripped open a large, square box. An action scene with a masked man with a black hat and a sword was on it: Zorro! Jack put on his mask and hat. The sword was long and flexible, with a piece of chalk at the end. Zorro always left his "Z" as he confronted the evil-doers. Jack worked as hard as leaving his mark on walls, books, and clothes without breaking the chalk, as I had with my Ladder-Ball.

Earl was older and got older kids' stuff. He got a matching pen and mechanical pencil set, a compass for his upcoming "Silver Beaver" hike, and a few other dumb things. Dumb, at least by Jack and my standards. Dad explained the Silver Beaver was a Boy Scout hike, Earl was a Life Scout, one rank before Eagle, and would take five days. They would hike 50 miles along the highway at the top of the mountains.

I was also in scouts and had earned my Star Scout rank,

two below Eagle. I'm not sure what happened on the trip. Earl completed the hike, got his medal, but both of us were soon out of scouts. Dad was a scout leader, and he no longer went to meetings either.

After we opened the presents, we would go to Mass, and from church, we would go over to Grandma and Grandpa Stoneman's. We would bring a ball and gloves and play catch in the driveway. For supper, we would all go in, wash our hands and sit around the large dining table. Whereas the Deppen's table was a relaxed come-and-go affair, the Stoneman's table was much more formal. We had roasted leg of lamb with mint jelly. Grandma and mom would boil, peel, and de-vein small cocktail shrimp. Grandma would make her own cocktail sauce, and the meal started with a shrimp cocktail. Mom always made a pie or two, which we had for dessert.

Grandma and grandpa only had a small tabletop tree with a few decorations. Cards from friends and relatives were on a ribbon strung along one wall. But the Christmas spirit was subdued. Earl and Jack would go to the bedroom and watch television on a small black and white set. The adults would play a game of Canasta, and I would watch. I would occasionally ask a few questions here and there. They would eventually feel comfortable enough with me to play their hand if they had to go to the bathroom or go to the kitchen to get a piece of pie, coffee, or milk.

By the time we finished the game and we were heading home, both Earl and Jack were fast asleep on the bed. The television station they had been watching had gone off the air, and the only thing on the television was static. We'd pile into the car. Earl and Jack would sleep all the way home. Me, I was wide awake, observing everything.

A lot of kids find riding in a car restful and often fell asleep. That was how it was for Earl and Jack. I would talk to myself, giving myself directions home, either from the Deppen's or from the Stoneman's. I had landmarks I watched for as we rode home.

It was a different story come sunrise. Earl and Jack were up at the crack of dawn, and it would take some time for the young eyes in my head to open and come alive.

A week later, we would be back at the Deppen's for New Year's Eve. At 9 pm exactly, grandma would call her family in Harrisburg, Pennsylvania, and wish them a Happy New Year. We would drive home only to be back early the next morning. Grandpa had, the day before, gotten a flatbed truck from work, put chairs on the back, and we waited for the Tournament of Roses Parade. We would leave shortly after the parade and get home so dad could listen to the Rose Bowl football game on the radio while tinkering in the garage. Mom would busy herself in the kitchen getting dinner ready. The three boys played with new toys and shared and compared our gifts with those the neighbors got.

School was out from December 23rd to January 1st. By early afternoon on Christmas day, we removed all the remnants of Christmas presents. New clothes had been put away, and new toys were taken to our rooms.

Our tree remained up until the Saturday after New Year's Day, as did our outside lights. It was my job to help mom take off and box the Christmas ornaments. Earl and Jack helped dad take down and put away the outside lights. In the hallway, we had a crawl space. One of us would bring the ladder from the garage, and dad would slide the crawlspace cover to the side. Dad was on the ladder, and Earl would hand him the boxes of Christmas ornaments and lights that Jack and I had given him. Our attic was our storage area. Once this was done, Christmas was officially over.

January 2nd came, and everything returned to normal. Mom and dad were back at work, and the three of us were back in school. But the new year would be anything but normal. I would have my first experience with the death of a friend.

10

The Funeral

THE FUNERAL

Growing up, I never attended a funeral. Oh, I knew people who had died. My Aunt Pauline was 102 when she died, and I remembered my parents going to her funeral. According to my parents, children did not go to funerals. My Great Aunt "Antie" had arthritis and had a stroke. She lived in a house trailer around the corner from my grandparents, and I remember going by one day, and there was no one home. I was told she died.

I had other aunts and uncles pass away from everything from old age to auto accidents and even suicide. My parents would go to the funeral, and the three of us would stay home. I once made the macabre joke that the first funeral I would attend would be mine. It has turned out not to be true, but funerals were and are mystical and mysterious.

Being Catholic, we had an Extreme Unction, known today as Last Rites, crucifix over the door to our house. In it, we kept a bottle of water the priest would bless, making it holy water. There were also two candles, which were part of the ritual. Every once in a while, mom would get the crucifix down, open it up and put more water in the vile. We knew we would use the contents only when someone died, but that was still an abstract concept.

During my sophomore year in high school, death and funerals permanently lost their abstractness. On a Saturday evening along Arrow Highway, a busy highway south of town, two cars with teens were racing. Just as now, this was an illegal event that many watched. A tire blew, and the cars collided. There were three boys in one car, two in the other. Their speed was more than 70 miles per hour. Seat belts, collapsible steering columns, energy-absorbing frames, and seat belts were not yet part of the automobile.

When the tire blew, it caused the cars to slam together, and they bounced. One went sideways into a light pole, the other rolled several times, coming to rest on its roof. Both engines continued to roar until the gas no longer flowed. Two passengers were tossed about within the car and were ejected. One out the side window and the other through the windshield. All were from the same family. They were cousins. The boys in each car were brothers.

The news rippled through the high school on Monday. David Vee was the only one I knew. We had several classes together in high school and were in the same class in junior high. He was fun to be around and a star on the track team. He was short, wiry, and speedy. A good student, he had an effervescent personality and was generally described as funny.

David was the first person my age to die. The five were to have a common funeral and be buried together at Post Oak Catholic Cemetery. Five identical mahogany caskets held their bodies and were transported from the funeral home by five identical, white hearses. I attended catechism each Wednesday night at St. Francis Catholic School, next to St. Francis of Rome Catholic Church. The Wednesday evening following the accident, a rosary was to be said in honor of Martin, David, Richard, Miguel, and Peter. The five Vee boys that died in that awful accident.

I watched from a distance as the five identical hearses arrived. Each pulled up to the front of the church, and a group of men came and carried the caskets, one by one, into the church. Nearby lights bounced off the sheen of each box.

I was Catholic, and I was friends with David and knew the other boys. But I was not Mexican, which was to be a traditional Mexican funeral, said in Spanish. The rosary was to start at 7:30 pm. My catechism ended at seven. It was my intention to go to the rosary and say goodbye to my friend. Even if said in Spanish, I knew the rosary and could say with them in English.

Their mothers, sisters, aunts, and grandmothers were all crying loudly. I could hear them as I approached the church. Having never been to a funeral, their wails increased my nervousness and fear for what I would experience. Would the caskets be open or closed? What would I say? What would I do? I started the short walk to the church several times but never made it.

Fear won out. I did not want to go in where there was obviously so much pain. Many of the parents of my friends of Mexican descent spoke little or no English. I was in virgin territory without a coherent plan of action. Would they even understand what I was saying?

After all, they had carried the bodies into the sanctuary, and the doors closed, I stood by one of the white hearses. Tears welled up and began running down my cheek. I said a Lord's Prayer and a Hail Mary quietly, head bowed while facing the church. When I finished, without looking up, I said in a quiet whisper, "David, I will miss you."

When I got home, I talked with my mother about my experience. She put her arms around me tried to comfort me. "It's probably best you didn't go in," she whispered while still holding me. "You don't want to intrude on a family's time of grief. But, David, knew you were there, and he heard your prayers."

I hope she was right. I missed David. Before graduating, more classmates would die and I never went to their funerals either. Sometimes, we were at different high schools at the time of their death, and I wouldn't learn about their passing until later. Others were just kids that I knew attended my school, but I did not personally know them. None the less, each time I learned of the passing of someone I knew or knew of, I would offer the two most sacred prayers of the Catholic church – the Lord's Prayer and the Hail Mary.

Music was always a great neutralizer. When I was happy, music helped me share that excitement and energy. On the other hand, when I could cope with the bad things life gave me through my music.

11

Spade Cooley, Cliffie Stone, and the Tijuana Jail

SPADE COOLEY, CLIFFIE STONE, AND THE TIJUANA JAIL

Music is and has always been a big part of my life. While I was growing up, there was always music in the house. Dad has his records going out in the garage. Mom either had records playing or at least the radio playing while she did housework. The old folks loved "The Lawrence Welk Show," and teens had "American Bandstand." I actually enjoyed both. I felt I was from another generation because I loved Teresa Brewer, Kay Starr, Patti Page, and others who were not of the rock-and-roll era. I also loved the current crop of pop stars.

We lived five houses up from the city line. When dad was giving directions to our house, he had to ask from where they were coming. If they came one way, they had to turn right on Broadway. If they came from the opposite direction, they had to the left onto Gladstone. It was the same street. The north side of the road was Gladstone, while the south side of the road was Broadway.

Valleydale was an unincorporated housing development

on the south side of the street. At one time, it was a vegetable farm, and I can remember very clearly the day the white ambulance from White's Funeral Home showed up and took a worker to the hospital. He was picking strawberries when a rattler stuck and got him in the hand. Later, the need for houses outweighed the need for rattlesnake infested fields. The vegetable farm was replaced with new homes and an extensive park with an amphitheater.

Each Saturday night, there was a barn dance, but without the barn. Country swing was king, and live music could be heard from the park's amphitheater every Saturday night. The first major recording artist I ever saw was at this park. Spade Cooley was a big shot on the country swing circuit.

Unfortunately, Spade remembered today not for his music, but for an argument he had with his wife. It did not end well for her. During the fight, Cooley pulled out a pearl-handled six-shooter revolver and shot her to death. One did not do the job, and according to news reports, emptied the gun. They found Spade guilty of first-degree murder, but he never served a day in prison. You see, Spade is also remembered for his sentencing hearing. The judge sentenced Spade to life in prison. Then the great Spade Cooley got a strange look on his face, grabbed his chest, looked at his lawyer, and dropped dead of a heart attack. Right there in the courtroom. In front of the judge, God and everybody. He literally dropped dead!

The most frequent band, however, was Cliffie Stone's. He didn't have the name or clout that Cooley commanded, but Stone was the hands-down favorite in our neck of the woods. Our next-door neighbor, Warren, worked at a grocery distribution warehouse in Los Angeles during the day and played in swing bands at night and on weekends. These bands included Cliffie Stone's.

The house on the other side was a rental. The neatest thing about that house was an arbor covered with concord grapevines. We always made sure we were friends with the people living there, and when it was vacant, who cared? Either way, we would often come home with purple stains from the grapes.

Juan Padilla and his family lived there for a while. They are the first family I remember living there. Juan was the head gardener at a famous Southern California racetrack. Juan's yard was impeccable. On Saturday, they invited us over for a traditional Mexicana dinner. It was the first time I had ever had a taco, refried beans, or a jalapeno.

"Where's the silverware?" dad asked.

Juan simply held up a tortilla chip and demonstrated its use in scooping up the beans and salsa; he called chili,

They had one son, Pete. One day, his cousin, a Maria with long, flowing black hair and obviously confused and frustrated, confronted Pete.

"What kind of Mexican are you? Whoever heard of a blue-eyed, blonde Mexican?"

Many Mexicans lived in our little town, and all of them were dark-haired and brown-eyed. Pete, however, indeed did have blue eyes and blonde hair.

The people that moved in after the Padilla's left was just man and wife. He would sit on the patio and play his guitar. I got to know him pretty well and learned his name was Denny

Thompson. He was a professional songwriter. The Kingston Trio could be heard on the radio singing his song, "The Tijuana Jail." He played two versions. One version was the song he wrote. When the song was published and record by The Kingston Trio and others, they kept the words but put them to an old folk tune in the public domain. Luckily, Thompson got to retain sole writing credits. Since the record sold more than a million copies, it made him a lot of money.

One Saturday, all three households were in Warren's living room having a jam session. There was discussion about who wrote "Ten Little Bottles" and laden with stories of songs, singers, and songwriting. It was a fascinating afternoon.

Not long after that, a new family moved into the house. Denny Thompson and his wife moved. Thanks to the royalties from "The Tijuana Jail," Denny and his wife could build a new home in Charter Oak, near Mount San Antonio College, Mount SAC for short. Denny was to be teaching music in the fall.

After the Thompson's moved out, the house remained vacant. Jack and I would continue to sneak over and pick the grapes. An older couple moved in and tore out the grapes. We never really got to know them, but they did not like grapes. One weekend, they took down the arbor and dug up the grapevines. They were nice enough, but we missed the grapes.

Soon after the new neighbors moved in, mom and dad decided they wanted a smaller yard and bought a house in West Covina, ten miles to the south of Azusa. It was on a hill, and only the houses on the hill were in West Covina. All the houses at the base and across the highway were in Covina.

Within a year, I would be a high school graduate and would enlist in the Navy. My parents lived there until they passed away. It was their home, and they had many friends there. It was, however, never really my home.

While still living in Azusa, our family would continue to have our little dramas and adventures. Sometimes these little dramas were real and needed to be handled. Most of the time, however, it was just a case of a misunderstanding.

12

The Day my Brothers Died

THE DAY MY BROTHERS DIED

Azusa, "Everything from A to Z in the USA," is nestled at the San Gabriel Mountain's foothills. Famed highway U.S. Route 66 is its primary east-west axis, while California 39 is its north-south axis. Established by Sunkist Growers in the 30s and 40s, we knew Azusa for its many orange groves, along with a few groves of lemons and limes. There was a time when to build a home or a school, you had to cut down a grove of citrus fruit trees.

Azusa was primarily a bedroom community to the greater Los Angeles area. The Los Angeles Transit Authority operated a streetcar, The Red Car, that ran to Azusa twice a day. Early in the morning, it would pick up and carry them deep inside the bowels of Los Angeles County. Twelve hours later, at 6 in the evening, it would return them home to their families.

Azusa had three primary industries. Jet engines were just coming into play as a viable engine for aircraft. Aerojet-General built the engines in Azusa. Several times a week, you could hear the roar as test engines came to life. Like a good neighbor,

Aerojet, as the locals called the plant, would invite all the children from a selected neighborhood to the plant at Christmas for a party. They would then give each child a gift. They chose a different neighborhood each year, so they had invited every neighborhood in the city to a party at Aerojet every five or six years.

At the base of the mountains was Foothill Dairy, supplying fresh milk to much of the San Gabriel Valley's eastern portion. Aromatic, local schools would annually show up for a tour of the facility and some fresh milk. Occasionally, schools would travel further inward to Bosco's, a goat dairy for some real goat's milk. However, it was Foothill Dairy that made its presence known to residents on the north side of town.

The third employer was more secretive. A high fence with barbed wire at the top surrounded a large (to a small boy) building with lots of windows. Signs abounded with the simple phrase, U.S. NAVY – KEEP OUT. The facility built torpedoes. Ten miles into the mountains was another naval facility with the same signage. A ramp was visible, and it was a torpedo testing facility.

Other than that, Azusa was a quiet town. Nothing much happened there except for three things. I lived on the south side of town, and just across the busy highway was a strawberry farm. If you were brave enough, you could dart across the highway and grab a few strawberries. I think they planned on this as nothing was ever said. One day, workers were working when suddenly, the ambulance from White's Funeral Home, in the 50s and 60s, the funeral homes were often the ambulance providers, showed up with lights flashing and siren blaring. A worker had bent down to pick the strawberries and did not see the rattler coiled up just inches from the fruit. When the worker bent to pick the strawberry, the snake struck and got him in the hand.

The second infamous incident was the fire at the feed store. On Azusa Avenue, California 39, at the streetcar track, was a feed store. One afternoon in July, with temperatures near or at the century mark, the hay caught fire and the wooden structure went up in smoke. The thick black smoke could be seen for miles. My grandmother was doing some shopping in Monrovia, about ten miles west of Azusa, would later tell us even she could see the smoke from the fire.

The third incident attributed to Azusa actually happened at Crystal Lake, twenty-five miles into the mountains above Azusa. Three teenagers had been brutally murdered and beheaded. They found their heads in a campground out-house. The bodies were never found, nor was the murderer. This was about when they were building the new interstate highways in Los Angeles County, and many locals surmised the bodies were now part of the newly completed San Bernardino Highway, now known as I-10.

Calling Crystal Lake, a lake would be an exaggeration. The state stocked it with rainbow trout, and there was a ranger's office there. However, any boat bigger than a rowboat or canoe would have found the facility woefully inadequate. There were times during summer droughts, one could just about walk across the lake without being in water over their head – if you were about six feet tall. A pre-teen at five-five, it was always over my head.

One summer, my family and my aunt and uncle spent a long weekend at Crystal Lake. My dad and Rodney liked to fish and would spend hours along the shoreline. My dad was the better fisherman, and yet between them, it took most of the afternoon to catch enough fish to feed eight of us. My mom and her sister would talk, drink tea and walk among the wildflowers. They managed to find small jars here and there, and when we sat down to eat at the picnic table, there would be flowers to make the dinner festively formal.

Rodney's youngest, Mikey, was Jack's age and was adventurous. And like my younger brother, a little on the mischievous side. While my brothers and I were playing on the beach and, occasionally, ventured out into the lake itself, Mike found a tree with limbs low enough for him to reach. Taking advantage of the situation, he hoisted himself onto the limb and began climbing the tree. He was maybe fifteen feet up when he paused.

"This tree is so easy to climb, I wonder if a bear has ever climbed it?" He said this out loud, but mostly to himself as there was no one else around him. At about that time, he heard a strange noise and felt the tree moving. A little worried, he managed to glance down at the precise time a black bear cub was climbing HIS tree and graining ground.

"Bear! Bear!" he kept hollering. "Bear! Bear!" which got the attention of pretty much everyone. Our parents. Other campers. But especially the bear cub below him. Both stopped, looked at one another, and both decided simultaneously to get down. My brothers and I came over to see what the commotion was all about, and we saw both Mikey and the bear descend the tree. As we would tell the story later, Mikey was a good ten feet above the bear when he realized what was happening and shimmied down the tree so fast, he beat the bear to the ground.

The boy hightailed it to the campsite and the comfort of his mother, who was both happy and mad to see him. The bear had copied Mikey and ran in the opposite direction to his mother, who, herself, did not look all that pleased with the situation.

After lunch, my brothers and I decided to take a hike. Mikey had said that he had had enough excitement for one day. So, my older brother Earl, my younger brother Jack, and I went off walking. I was naïve and gullible and pretty much accepted what Earl told me. As we walked, we would pass some deep ravines, and Jack and I would pick up stones and toss them down. We would aim at a boulder or a bush, and neither of us was an excellent shot.

"Be careful, you two," said Earl. "You don't want to slip."

"Why? There's nothing there but bushes and rocks," and Jack threw another stone.

"And snakes!"

Did I say I was afraid of snakes? Well, I am, and so two things happened. First, I quit throwing the rocks. And I began to look for snakes. I was sure I could see one or two down among the underbrush and boulders.

"If you fall down there, the snakes will come and get you. They'll bite you, and you'll die before anyone can get to you."

That was enough for me. I backed off the ridge of the ravines another six inches. But Jack? No, the story just made what he was doing more exciting. Exciting for all of us as we told each other snake stories and how we could actually see snakes down in the ravine. Then Jack slipped and went tumbling down. He landed in a bunch of bushes and quickly disappeared. You could hear some stones still cascading down, which I just knew snakes were going after my brother.

Without hesitation, Earl was down at the bush, and he too was out of sight. Both brothers are now down among the snakes, both out of sight, both dead. Or would be before I could get help. Mad, angry, and scared, I ran back to camp. I was wailing and crying, and when I reached the campsite, my mother ran up to me.

"Honey. What's wrong? Where are your brothers? Where's Earl and Jack" She was asking so many questions so quickly, I couldn't get the answer to the first one out before she was asking a second, third, fourth . . .

"They're dead." And began crying again, only harder this time.

Mom screamed, my aunt came and held me. My dad and my uncle came running. When mom told them what I had said, they took off in the direction from which I had come. They hadn't gone too far when they heard boys talking and laughing. A few minutes later, everyone was back safe and sound in the campground.

It befuddled my dad. He was relieved that Jack and Earl were OK, but mad as the devil himself that they made me believe anyone falling into the ravines would be killed. We got a stern talking to, and they confined us to the campground for the rest of the afternoon.

That night, I figured we were pretty much out of trouble. Jack thought it was a hoot that I got so scared. Earl got upset because he knew how gullible I was and let me believe the story he was telling. He got yelled at by both mom and dad. But, as we lay in the tent in our sleeping bags, I could hear my parents and my aunt and uncle talking about the afternoon's adventures: the bear, the snakes, and the deaths. They were laughing. I fell asleep confident that when I awoke in the morning, all would be well.

Mikey was not the only one to have a close encounter with a bear. Earl was sleeping late the next morning when he felt someone or something tickling his foot. He sat up, hollered the now familiar phrase, “Bear!” and jumped out of bed. A bear cub had found something enticing about Earl’s foot and was licking it. Looking back, it was a pretty amusing sight.

Earl was not, however, the only one to have an encounter with a wild animal, though mine was smaller.

POP GOES THE WEASEL

Growing up, a lot of our friends had pets. Of course, Earl had his parakeet, Peaty, but we didn't really have a pet. The Ackers behind us had a couple of dogs. Mr. Ackers worked for Kenosha Auto Transport and found a small brown dog wandering around the yard one day. It had apparently hitched a ride on one of the auto transports. He named the dog "Butch," and it could be a mean dog. They posted "Beware of Dog" on their fences and kept the dog either tied up or in the house when they came to read the electric meters.

Butch would show his teeth and growl at any stranger who came around. If Richard or one of his brothers was with the intruder, Butch was your typical friendly pet. However, Butch was protective of his territory, and no one wanted to venture into their backyard alone.

There was one exception, me. Richard was my age, and we were in the same grade and had the same teacher. He was frequently over at our house, or we were over at his. They lived directly behind us, and we would climb their fence coming and going. Butch was so used to me being over there that when I climbed the fence, he alerted the family of my presence and came running over to be petted.

The Lewis family lived a couple of houses up the street on the other side. Their yard was marked by a gigantic Christmas tree in the front yard. They planted it one Christmas but planted it too close to the house. As it grew, it became increasingly difficult to reach the front door by the walkway from the driveway. I was a frequent visitor, and Brenda, who was in my class at Rhoades Avenue, would listen to the dramatic radio shows. They didn't have a television. They also had two beautiful collies and raspberry bushes in the backyard. When it came time to pick berries, they always invited me to help pick them. They also had various fruit trees, so the Stoneman's were never without fresh fruits.

The Lewis's were from Kansas and would go back east to visit family every year. It would be my job to take care of the dogs. I visited them at least twice a day and made sure they had food and water. I played with them, and it was a lot of fun.

Warren, next door, had rabbits and chickens, but they were not pets. Occasionally he would kill a rabbit or a chicken for dinner. He even shared the animals with us, and we would have fresh chicken and rabbit once a month or so.

Earl's best friend, Jerry, had the most unusual pet. He kept it in a cage in their garage. It was a raccoon he had named Rocky. Rocky was fun to watch, and I even got to touch him one time. The only time Rocky was out of the cage was when the garage doors were closed. Jerry tried to let Rocky play in the backyard but soon learned Rocky was adventurous. It took Jerry and Earl more than an hour to recapture Rocky after one of his escapades.

We had a couple of dogs. Blackie was a short, black dog we took care of for a while and thought about keeping him. Dad eventually said no, and we gave him back. Blackie belonged to a friend of my dad who was retiring and moving. He was trying to find a new home for Blackie.

Suzie was a brown and white springer spaniel we got as a puppy. She was loving and playful, and we all adored her. We did not know about distemper or how bad a disease it was for dogs. I came home from school for lunch and found the dog catcher loading Suzie into her truck. Mom explained that Suzie was sick and would not be coming back.

The owner of the most unusual pet, however, was me. I also hold the record for having the pet for the shortest period. I think I had Weasel, the weasel; I didn't have it long enough to give it a proper name for about three hours.

I was sitting on the back porch one summer afternoon when this flash of brown fur ran across the yard. It ran to the side of the garage and was caught between the chain-link fence of our neighbors and the garage. Dad got a bucket and gave me one. We each had a cover, so when the thing, we didn't know yet what we had, ran into the bucket, we could capture it.

Once caught, we discovered it was a small, furry weasel. Dad quickly made a cage out of some plywood and wire mesh. Did you know a weasel can chew through wood and wire? It chewed a hole in the wood, which we patched up as quickly as we found it. We gave it some lettuce and carrots from the refrigerator.

Weasel had settled down, and we thought we were safe. We put the cage in the shade of a large sycamore tree, and we went inside for lunch. We came back to find the wood near the top of the cage gnawed, and the wire mesh pushed up a bit. Weasel? Well, he was nowhere to be found, and we never saw it again.

We were city dwellers, and rarely ventured into the mountains. Especially in winter where all sorts of things could and did happen.

AND AWAY WE GO

Wrightwood is a resort in the San Bernardino Mountains about 40 miles west of Mount San Antonio, more affectionally known for its bald granite dome as Mount Baldy. There are campgrounds everywhere for those brave enough to pull a trailer up the winding road or those rugged enough to actually sleep in a tent in the summer. For those softies, there are a limited number of rooms at the lodge.

The resort is high enough to capture a sufficient amount of snow to attract skiers and others who like to play in the snow in the wintertime. Although I prefer the mountains over the beach, I have never been skiing. I took a trip to Mount Baldy's ski resort during the summer to learn skiing rudiments, but we skied on straw. My family came up to Wrightwood, one of the many resorts on Mount Baldy, one winter but had to settle for fake snow. When the temperature is low enough, they put a rainbird, a pulsating sprinkler, on, and it shoots water into the air, it freezes and comes down as snow.

Earl and his friend Jerry came up here one weekend to try their hand at tobogganing. The snow was about three or four feet deep with more on the way. Now Earl is approaching six feet and weighs a paltry 185 pounds. Jerry is just over six feet and weighs closer to 250 pounds. That means that when the two of them are on the toboggan, there are 335 pounds of weight on that wooden sled.

The two of them spent hours going down the slopes and having a wonderful time. Only on the steepest hill did they get any air when hitting a lift in the terrain. Earl knew our family had talked about coming up for some winter fun and though the tobogganing would be an excellent adventure.

Over dinner, Earl went on and on and on about their experience. Just when we thought Earl was finished and someone else could speak, he would think of something else and there went another five minutes.

"And where exactly were you," quizzed dad.

"Campground two. Just next to the lodge dining hall," explained Earl, as if we all knew exactly where that dining hall was.

"Did you go flying?" was mom's concern.

"Only on the last run. The steepest hill with the fastest speeds and then only for a split second." He continued, "We tried, but we couldn't get the thing to fly more than a few feet."

"Sounds like fun," Jack chimed in thinking about Earl's assessment.

Dad was quiet for a moment. Without looking at anyone, he said, "We can head up there Saturday, and let Bruce and Jack can try tobogganing."

Now, I am not exactly afraid of speed or thrills. At the same time, my concerns are well known in the family. I don't like the big roller coasters, but I always enjoyed the smaller "Wild Mouse" ride at the L.A. County Fair. I like the Ferris wheel, where you pull on the lever, and you travel over the top upside down. I just don't like things that make my mind think we're out of control. Unlike Jack, I was not particularly excited to try tobogganing.

We arrived at Wrightwood just after noon. We got something hot to drink and a hot dog.

Excitedly, Earl said, "I'll get the toboggan," and ran off toward the rental shed.

He soon came back with a wooden sled, no skids, a curved upfront, rope handles on the side, and some rope upfront that gave the false impression that we could steer this thing.

"What hill do you recommend?" inquired dad.

"The little one over there is fun."

Dad cautiously asked, "And you don't go flying?"

Jack and I got on this thing. It was about six feet long and intended for more than two people, at least in my mind it was.

"Get on, and I'll push you off," said Earl with an air of excitement in his voice.

I got in first, and Jack got in behind me. Both Earl and Jerry were close to six feet tall and put 300 plus pounds on their sled, Jack and I were pretty even in height, and that put us at about five-five for each of us. Even with all of our heavy coats, we did not put more than 240 pounds on the toboggan together.

"Ready . . . Set . . :" Earl pushed before he said go. The two went down a clear path. The ride was bumpy but not uncomfortable. Then, we hit an uptick in the terrain, and all three of us, the toboggan, Jack, and I went flying at least 30 feet down the slope. We hit with a thud. Jack did not have a firm grip, and when we hit terra firma, Jack fell off the back and onto his back and bounced a couple of times before coming to rest. Me, well I hung on for dear life, eyes closed, teeth clenched and fell hard on my back, still on the toboggan for another ten feet before we came to a rest.

"Hey, that was fun. Let's do it again!" Jack was saying as he came up to where I had come to a rest. Still on my back with my eyes shut.

"It's OK, Bruce. It's stopped. You can sit up." It was my mom reassuring me.

"Won't go flying, eh?"

"Well," Earl mumbled, "I guess Jerry and I had a few more pounds."

"Well, it was fun to watch, and I think your brothers had fun."

The next ride down, I was on the back, and we hit a different lift, and when we came down hard, I lost my grip and slid off the back. Mom and dad, Bill and Jack, and various other combinations took turns riding down the hills. Mom and dad even took the only hill that gave Earl and Jerry air going down. When they hit the left, they were in their air for only a few seconds but long enough to travel 20 feet down the slope. I even rode it a couple of more times just to get my brothers to be quiet.

We stopped at a Bob's Big Boy for hamburgers in Pomona on the way home. Although we all agreed that we had fun, we never went back. Not even Earl and Jerry ever went back. Oh, we went to Wrightwood a couple of times in the summer. Generally, we were taking a ride, and dad enjoyed the mountains, so we stopped and ate lunch at the lodge. But that was our one and only wintertime family outing.

Church has always been important to me. Even as kids, wc always went to church.

13

The Gospel According to Schwinn

THE GOSPEL ACCORDING TO SCHWINN

We grew up in the Roman Catholic Church. Earl and I were known as "Cradle Catholics," having been baptized as infants. For whatever reason, Jack was not baptized until he was in junior high. It makes this even more curious when you realize they named Jack after mom's best friend's brother, who is a priest!

Grandpa Stoneman was a Free Mason. I know this because of the ring he always wore. He said very little about it. Dad told some. There were some hostilities between the Masons and Roman Catholics, much like mixing oil and water. They just don't mix. Other than this mysterious connection, I don't remember them being affiliated with any particular denomination or ever attending church.

Mom grew up in the Episcopalian church. I know her parents went to church often. Mom's best friend in high school was Roman Catholic, and mom converted while she was in high school. Dad converted when they got married. I do not think dad's family was happy with this conversion, especially with the riff between Masons and Catholics; however, The Deppen's were just happy Mom and Dad went to church.

The family would get up early on Sunday mornings and head off to mass. Taking communion meant we went to the earliest mass. To take communion, we had to go to confession on Friday or Saturday and not eat or drinking anything other than water from midnight on Saturday until communion on Sunday.

Catholics could not eat meat on Fridays, so we would have many vegetable plates, macaroni and cheese, and fish. One staple was a carrot and raisin salad. On Friday, after a particularly trying week, dad looked at the salad and said, "Flies!" He repeated himself and grew louder with each repeat. "I've been around flies all week," he said rather loudly. "I do not expect to come home and have flies for dinner!" We never had that dish again.

We ate lots of fish. Grandpa Deppen was a sports fisherman and would occasionally drive down to Ensenada, Mexico, and bring back sailfish, swordfish, yellowtail, and various other species. He would cut the fish up, and each family would get their share. Sometimes, Earl got to go with him, and they brought back a swordfish on their first trip together.

However, we were not Catholics exclusively. The Catholic Church had catechism each Wednesday evening. When we were in elementary school, the church would park a trailer outside of school. In the last hour on Wednesdays, Catholic students would receive religious instruction in the trailer. However, Catholics did not have a vacation Bible school, even though Catholic mothers struggled just as hard to find things for their children to do during the summer. The Seventh Day Adventist Church held a VBS in nearby Irwindale. Mom would take us in the morning and pick us up after lunch in the afternoon.

The church was smaller than St. Francis of Rome, where we were on Sunday mornings. It also had two large shade trees, so it always seemed cool. The best part, they let us climb the trees. Just before lunch, we would have chapel service. They had an old pump organ that the player could pump air with two pedals. Or, you could have someone behind the wall and pump the bellows to activate the reeds. All the boys, and including Jack and me, had the opportunity to pump the bellows.

Although we would almost always attend mass, Jack and I would occasionally attend the little green church on First Street. The sign outside said, "Friends Church." KTTV, an independent station broadcasting from Pasadena, would travel among six or eight churches and televise their service. When it came to The Friend's church's turn to broadcast their service, Jack and I got to go to the little green church on the corner and watch the big cameras. Mom would say she saw us on television, even we were not within camera range. It was just exciting to be a part of a live television broadcast.

As we got older, mom and dad would stay in bed and send us off to mass. I don't think it was a matter of mom and dad drifting from the church as much as they needed time to themselves. Earl was now living with Grandma and Grandpa Deppen, so they just needed to get Jack and me out of the house.

Mom and dad smoked, and Jack would sneak a couple of cigarettes out of an open pack. Anyone could buy tobacco products. We would buy a cigarillo or a Swisher Sweet cigar, saying it was for our parents, but who would never see them. Instead of heading to church, we would head over to the park and light up. Jack took to it almost immediately. I did not find it enjoyable. Who wants to intentionally put a fire in their mouth? I tried the "Cool and refreshing taste of Kool cigarettes." It was a lie. It was still a fire in the mouth, only with a hint of mint flavoring. I did not like my mouth on fire, and I never really took up smoking. I would occasionally take a puff of someone's cigarette but never became a smoker. On the other hand, Jack became a smoker to the extent our parents had to start hiding their cigarettes.

Mom and dad, obviously suspecting something and began asking for a bulletin from the church. Then they would ask which priest was saying mass. One Sunday, while Jack and I thought we were safe, we picked up the bulletin and watched to see which priest was saying mass. When we got home, we got the usual questions. We didn't know; mom and dad were at mass and saw neither of us nor our bikes. We proffered the bulletin as usual and proclaimed Father Duggan as the priest saying mass. They changed the question this Sunday, and they asked who delivered the sermon.

That Sunday was "State of the Church" Sunday. Father Barrett delivered a report on the finances of the church and other information. He delivered this information, and he did not appear until it was time for scripture reading. He read the scripture and gave his report. By that time, Jack and I were at the park. We were toast!

They still allowed us to go to mass alone, but besides providing a bulletin, give a recap of the sermon. So much for sneaking off for a smoke.

My senior year in high school added a new chapter to my religious training. The bishop was coming to confirm a new class. Although this generally happened in upper elementary years, neither Jack nor I had been confirmed. I had seen my orchestra teacher at mass a couple of times, and we talked about the bishop's visit. It surprised him I had not confirmed, and he offered to stand up for me. Another friend of mine stood up for Jack, and we were confirmed during my senior year and Jack's sophomore year.

Throughout my formative years, either Jack Daniels or Jim Beam would, on occasion, attempt to get me to become a priest. Led by mom's best friend, Julie, who converted her to Catholicism, and Jack was named after Julie's brother who was a priest, I would be ushered into the bedroom where there was a phone and calls would be made on my behalf to get me into the seminary. This never happened early in the evening. Generally, it was around the time mom was rounding us up to hit they hay, and always after they had more than a few Coca Colas laced with either Jack or Jim. As if on cue, mom would come in, take the phone from Julie and assure me that I was not destined for the priesthood.

After high school, I continued attending church but grew disenchanted with the Catholic church. During one catechism lesson, the issue of Free Masons came up. I was told to have as little contact with my grandfather because he was a Mason. They taught us only Catholics went to heaven. To me, a loving Father would welcome all his children, not just those from a specific neighborhood. However, I have always gone to church.

However, both Earl and Jack decided church was not their bag, and they stopped going to church altogether. Earl got married and he and his new wife continued searching for a church home but eventually quit looking and drifted away. Once we were confirmed, I think Jack gave up on church.

Over the years, Jack and I, collectively or individually, were believed to be responsible for things that went bump in the night. Either newly painted boards falling over or miles appearing mysteriously dad's car's odometer. Whatever it is we might or might not have done, nothing involved matches, lighters or fire.

14

We Didn't Start the Fire

WE DIDN'T START THE FIRE

The San Fernando and the San Gabriel valleys enjoy very similar weather patterns. The San Fernando and San Gabriel mountains block a lot of the hot air from the Mojave Desert to the north while capturing the cool ocean breezes from the south and west. No matter how hot it gets during the day, a cool evening is often the norm.

Earthquakes are an accepted way of life in Southern California. They occur so frequently, most people ignore the little ones. There are occasional severe quakes that damage houses and roadways built before they establish earthquake resistance codes. However, for kids, most earthquakes were nothing more than a minor inconvenience.

We would be riding our bikes when a quake would hit. The good thing is an earthquake is generally short-lived, and it is over in less than a minute. Riding down the street, as long as we were not showing off, there would be a brief period of instability—however, nothing to worry about. Showing off and riding with no hands, balancing the bike, and steering it with our bodies would present a unique set of problems. This often with a mad grab for the handlebars before crashing.

Sometimes, we would sit on the curb with our bikes on their kickstands. There would be this almost inaudible rumble, a brief shake, and our bikes would fall over. Then we knew we had just experienced a quake. We would laugh and pick up our bikes, then return to our spot on the curb.

Jack and I shared a bedroom, and we had bunk beds. Jack always liked the top bed, and that is where he was one Saturday morning when we had a slightly more powerful quake than usual. The earthquake hit at the same moment Jack rolled over toward the side away from the wall. Ker-plop! Jack fell out of bed and wound up with a black eye.

When we went to bed the previous night, I fought sleep for as long as I could, and thus, when I fell asleep, I fell asleep. I could sleep through just about anything. When I woke up that morning and went to the kitchen, I found mom cradling Jack, who had fallen back to sleep with an apparent black eye.

"What happened?" I asked as I pointed to and examined Jack's injured eye.

"Fell out of bed."

"When?"

"About an hour ago."

"Why? How?"

"Didn't you feel the quake?"

"What quake?"

We had an earthquake about an hour ago. It rolled Jack out of bed, and he fell on the floor. I swear, Bruce, a firetruck with its siren going full blast could rumble through the house, and you'd sleep through the whole thing."

"Sorry," I muttered. "Is Jack going to be OK?"

"Yes," she said with a smile. "Only his pride was really hurt."

Although earthquakes happened throughout the year, we really paid little attention to them except during the summer, when we were outside a lot.

The hot air from the desert and the cool breeze from the ocean would occasionally clash, and we would have a gully-washer of a storm. Azusa had several gullies in the 50s and 60s, which were favorite playgrounds. We could act out Tarzan and other exotic stories in this jungle-like environment. We were invincible and not afraid of anything: not Grass snakes or lizards or the like.

For a day or two after a summer thunder buster, these natural playgrounds were out of bounds. These were natural channels for the rainwater falling on the city and running down and out of the mountains. Los Angeles County would eventually take our playgrounds away. They put in concrete riverbeds to direct the runoff in the direction they wanted. This allowed for a more productive use of the land.

Occasionally, a lightning strike would hit dry timber, either dry pine needles on the ground or one of the gigantic redwoods or pine trees in the forest. Either way, the result was a forest fire that would bring out various resources. We would stand in the dark of night and watch the fires' glow from the safety of our houses.

In the morning, we would wake up and find a fine layer

of ashes on our cars, or on the water in our pools. Pasadena, Azusa or Pomona, whichever was at the base closest to the fire would receive the heaviest layer of ash. But it was not uncommon for people outlying areas such as Inglewood, Whittier or Chico to wake up to a light ash blanket as well.

One year, a pyromaniac drove from Mount Wilson north of Pasadena, across the mountain tops along the Angeles Crest Highway to Mount Baldy, north of San Bernardino. He set more than a dozen fires along the way. This was the most destructive fire to date and the most concerning to those of us below. The mountains were not a single range, but a series of mountain ranges close together. The lightning strikes would hit the second or third range, which had significantly higher peaks, and where there was the most snow in the winter. The Angeles Crest Highway Fire was set along the road near the top of the lowest and closest range.

We experienced fires' side effects in the spring when the many spring showers came and washed tons of scorched earth down the mountainsides. Mudslides in the second and third range posed little danger to life or property. However, slides on the lower peaks endangered both life and property. There are several campgrounds at these lower elevations, and some had year-round residents. If the slide did not directly damage the campgrounds, they often blocked roads, cutting off the residents' only access to food and fuel.

The technology was in its infancy during these trying times, and walkie-talkies were good for only short distances. It was hard-wired for communication between fire camps along the fire line and the control center in downtown Los Angeles.

So, when there was a fire, dad often had to spend weeks at a time at the fire providing necessary communication. During the Angeles Crest Fire, the fire jumped over the camp where dad was. Everyone had a fire blanket coated with aluminum that would not burn. One weekend, he came home and gave Jack and me his scorched fire blanket. He played down the danger he faced, but the look on mom's face told a different story.

There were no live video feeds of fires or other catastrophes. We relied on photographs printed in magazines and newspapers. One picture caught our attention. It was the first time I realized how dangerous my dad's job was. It was taken just moments before the fire jumped camp and scorched my dad's fire blanket.

I had a newfound respect for my dad and his bravery. One of the most important lessons I learned from my dad involved a work ethic. In addition to fires, dad would sometimes spend a week or two at one of the prisons near Palmdale. The one thing all three of learned from our dad was a solid work ethic. None of were afraid of working.

Earl worked at Burger Dan's around the corner from our house in Azusa, and Jack had his one paper route. For whatever reason, I turned out to be the workhorse of the three amigos.

MINIMUM WAGE

One of the easiest ways a kid could make money back in the 50s and 60s was to collect empty pop bottles. Depending on the size and brand, they would fetch either two cents or a nickel. We would go up and down the street, pulling a wagon and collecting bottles. We would then take them to the local corner store and cash them in. For a nickel, you could get a large Three Musketeer's bar that you could divide easily into three parts. Since a small bottle of Coke was only a nickel, you could buy one to wash down the candy.

I actually make more money collecting empty pop bottles for an hour than I did, making minimum wage crushing ice for my first job.

The biggest handicap to restaurants and cafeterias was ice. They needed it to keep cold food cool, but automatic ice machines were not commonplace and very expensive. My first actual job, at a whopping 35¢ an hour, was to crush ice and put it into ten-pound paper sacks. I did this for two or three hours on Wednesdays and Thursdays, depending on how much ice was needed.

A 200-pound piece of ice would roll out of the ice maker. It was scored for splitting into 25-pound cubes. So, with my ice pick and some ice tongs, I would cut a cube loose and run it through the chopper. Aero-Jet General was the largest employer in Azusa, and they had a cafeteria. The Azusa Ice Company provided them with a minimum of two dozen ten-pound sacks. They had an employee cafeteria food table lined with our ice.

The ice company also had a vending machine where you could put your quarter in the slot, and a 25-pound cube rolled out. Refrigerators used to be called iceboxes for a reason. My family had one/ The top two compartments were lined with a drainpipe, and we placed a 25-pound piece of ice in each compartment. The thick wood and aluminum lining slowed the melting process. Because cold air sinks, it cooled whatever was in the compartments below it. Unfortunately, I did not get an employee discount. My parents, just like everyone else, had to go to the vending machine and pay 25¢ for the block of ice. Eventually, Azusa Ice purchased one or two specially designed trucks and began making home deliveries. This was just about the time when iceboxes were being replaced with electric refrigerators.

I was one of those proverbial ninety-eight-pound weaklings. I worked out in the backyard with barbells and a Charles Atlas workbook. However, at 115 pounds soaking wet, I was not a muscle builder. I moved the blocks/bags of ice, using my right leg like a piston. I would do this so often that I developed a limp. Teachers were concerned that maybe I had hurt myself, but soon learned what my after-school job was and just smiled, saying, "Keep it up, gimpy!"

Almost all of us collected empty pop bottles for the instant gratification they provided. Still, a lot of kids made extra money mowing lawns. Especially if you had one of the new power mowers. We had two yards, the front, and the back. It was my job to mow and trim the front yard. Jack just had to mow the back. We didn't have one of those newfangled machines. Ours was a traditional mower that required muscle. Whether push or powered, these mowers worked similarly to a vacuum cleaner and rolled the grass clippings to the back. If you had a catcher, you stopped and emptied it into the compost pile every five minutes. If you didn't, you wound up with green tennis shoes. It was hard work, and it killed your weekends. Most kids mowed lawns on Saturdays as most also went to church on Sunday, and that was your weekend. Earl and Jack would mow a few lawns, but I found a more lucrative way to earn money.

In the 50s and 60s, people got most of their news from the newspaper. Radio gave headlines, and television news was still a public service relegated to a quarter-hour each evening. Even then, there were no sports stories, human interest angles, or weather reports. So, many kids became business people and independent distributors of weekly, morning, or afternoon newspapers from the local community, the region, or a close large city. I did it all. I delivered the hometown shopper that was free to the community and delivered weekly on Wednesday afternoons. Sometimes, my dad would load us in the back of his pickup, or mom in her car, and we'd toss the papers off the bed of the truck or out the back window of the car: Jack on one side of the car, I was on the other. As often as not, I would load the folded shoppers in my paper bags, two large canvas bags you could strap to a bicycle's handlebars, and off I'd go.

At one point, Jack and I both delivered the San Gabriel Valley Tribune. I had our street and the two streets behind. Jack had Vernon, Ellen, and Lemon, the three streets east of our street. Jack actually had more customers than I did, but I took longer to deliver the papers.

The paper was $1.75 a month, six days a week. We did not deliver on Saturdays. We each had a binder with a sheet with a year's worth of perforated receipts, one for each month. At the end of the month, we visited each house we delivered and collected. The route manager would deliver Friday's papers and collect what we owed him. Anything else was ours. Jack and I had to be responsible enough to keep track of our money. If we were short, our parents made up the difference, but then we had to pay them back. If we became habitually short, as Jack became, we gave up our route. I was never short or late with my payment.

The canvass bags we tied to our handlebars also had a hole in the center, and we could wear the bags as a vest, and the paper route walked. Once in a while, we would have a flat tire and did not have time to fix the flat, and so we slipped the bags over our heads and walked the route.

Jack was always a show-off and doing tricks with his bike. These tricks took a toll on both Jack and his bike. It would not be uncommon for Jack to have broken a wheel and could not use his bike to deliver the papers. Since he had further to go and had more customers, mom insisted I let Jack use my bike to deliver his papers, and I could walk my route. When we both rode bikes, Jack would get done fifteen to twenty minutes ahead of me. When I had to walk, it more like an hour after he got home that I finally made it.

At first, my parents thought maybe I was not doing the job correctly. They wondered if I was playing around rather than delivering papers. When the first month's subscriptions were collected, it became clear that the two of us were not equal. Jack focused on speed – how fast could he get his papers out. I focused more on service. I had customers who did not care if the paper was on the lawn or driveway. However, I had others who needed or requested the paper delivered on the porch, in a box, behind the storm door, or a few other odd places. I got to know my customers by name, and the reason I was late, I would visit with some of them along the way.

The papers sold for a dime, a quarter on the weekend. We paid a nickel for the daily papers and fifteen cents for the Sunday edition. They also gave us five extra papers to deliver to non-subscribers as an enticement to subscribe. Essentially, half of our monthly subscription went to the newspaper company, and half went to us. Any tips received were ours and neither reported to the company nor shared with them. Jack made his half and a little more. At the end of the month, I made another month's collection in tips.

At Christmas, Jack would receive some cards with an extra dollar inside. I got twice the number of cards Jack received, and more often than not, there was more than a dollar inside. My customers knew I was in the Boy Scouts, and I got a scout knife one year.

Jack started playing Little League and gave up his paper route. Until they could find a replacement for Jack's route, I did both but was very glad when I could just focus on my customers.

Pasadena Star-News and Morning Telegram wanted to expand their readership. Their papers were fifteen cents during the week and thirty cents on Sundays. Our cost was the same. I was approached, and I found I could handle both a morning and afternoon route. With the same number of customers each time, I could double my income and swapped out the Tribune for the two Pasadena papers. The route was a much larger area, and the first morning I was delivering, the police were curious and pulled me over. I was the first Pasadena

Telegram paperboy in the area, and the Tribune was an evening only paper. We talked for a few minutes, and I was on my way. For about two weeks, though, they kept me in-sight. I don't know if I worried them that I might get hurt or if they thought I had some sinister deed in mind. Eventually, they were satisfied with what I was doing, and my routine never varied. Every once in a while, I would spot them at a corner waiting on me. I'd wave, and they'd wave back.

New Year's Day in Pasadena is a huge deal. The Rose Parade, as the locals called it, or The Tournament of Roses, its official name, was a five-mile-long parade with floats covered entirely by flowers. When I was younger, my mom's dad would park a flatbed truck, nose in, and have chairs and risers on the back. The whole Deppen clan would magically appear and sit on the chairs and risers and watching the parade.

The Pasadena papers published a single edition on Sunday. If you were a morning subscriber or an afternoon subscriber, you got one copy of the paper. If you subscribed to both the morning and afternoon paper, you got a discount, however, only one Sunday paper. One year, the paper asked if I would like to sell papers at the parade. After talking it over with my parents, they agreed I could sell them. They would drop me off at a specified corner along Colorado Boulevard, the parade's main route.

They gave me fifteen papers, and on this day, they were fifty cents. Easier for me to make change. The papers cost me nothing, and however many papers I sold, that's how much money I made. I made $7.50 that morning, having sold out my total allotment. I sat on the curb with the other parade-goers and watched the parade.

My great uncle lived four or five blocks from where I was selling papers. They instructed me to would walk to their house. Mom said she would pick me up there, and if she wasn't there, my great aunt and uncle would watch me until she got there.

Paperboys did not last long in the business. Not that the work was hard, but they got cars, started playing sports, or discovered girls. Sometimes it was a mixture. We were not rich enough to have a second car, so I continued with the paper route. I wasn't athletic, and so sports did not enter the picture. Unfortunately, the best way to get a girl-friend was to have a car. Romance was never a deterrence. When I 'retired,' I was one of the oldest paperboys.

A classmate's dad worked for the Azusa Herald, a weekly paper. One of their regular paperboys wasn't watching where he was going and ran into the back of a car. Cars in those days were sheet metal and could not be easily damaged. Not so for the bike and its rider. This unfortunate lad broke his arm and could not deliver papers for two months, which stretched into four. I agreed to deliver the Azusa Herald each Wednesday afternoon while the regular carrier was on the mend. The only problem was, he got so he enjoyed not having to throw papers, and my stint continued until a full-time replacement could be found. A three-week temporary assignment lasted most of three months.

There was a benefit to being a successful paper boy. I became a successful entrepreneur. In different magazines aimed at kids, there was this advertisement to sell greeting cards to your neighbors. You sold a box of cards for a buck-twenty-five and kept seventy-five cents. I called on my neighbors, but also some of my best paper route customers. Unfortunately, my business did not last long. After all, a person could not use all the cards they purchased before the company wanted me to make repeat sales. I liked the money and job was fun, but I could not risk losing my paper route customers.

The last job I had while in high school came about from a friend of mine and my dad's friend. The friend's uncle had an apartment complex that was next to a new construction site. For about six months, he needed someone to keep the trash off his property, water and weed the shrubs and mow the lawn. There was a shed at the back of the property where a lawnmower and other tools were stored.

The job was in Baldwin Park, about 15 miles from home and two blocks from where a friend of my dad's lived. They both rode together to work, and dad would stop by, pick Pete up, and they'd head off to work. My job would be over before they got home, so I was to walk home when I got off work.

There was one unexpected benefit to the job. On Friday, dad and Pete would be home early, so dad said he could ride home with him. I walked to Pete's house, and there was this cute red-headed girl my age. She was friendly and talked for about five minutes. It wasn't until I got home that I learned the girl's name. When I asked her, all she said was, "Dodie."

When we got home, and at the dinner table, dad said, "Well, Bruce met a pop star today." I looked at him with a quizzical face. "Pete's babysitter is Dodie Stevens, and the two were talking when I got there to pick him up. Dodie Stevens had a record called "Pink Shoe Laces" playing on the radio. I did not know what she looked like, nor did I know she lived in Baldwin Park. I just blushed and smiled.

I got paid a flat rate of five bucks a day, which was extravagant for the period. They completed the construction next door in eight weeks, and so did my job. I was glad not to have to walk the fifteen miles home each day, and I learned I did not like solitary work. There wasn't anyone around, except the construction workers, during the day, which made the time go slowly.

My parents moved during my senior year, and I did not have a job during that time. My uncle got me a summer job that kept me away from home for two full months. My next job was in North Carolina, compliments of Uncle Sam and the Navy. I would visit as often as possible, but I never went back to live in Southern California.

In school we learned about nomadic people, those that moved from place to place. I identified with these people in that I walked anywhere and everywhere. Sometimes, I would travel familiar roads, other times it was new territory. As long as I could see the mountains, I knew I could not get lost.

15

Do You Know the Way?

DO YOU KNOW THE WAY?

Every winter, Boy Scouts would descend upon Victorville in the desert east of Los Angeles for Winter Jamboree. If you have ever watched old westerns, which were a staple of television in the 50s, and you saw Roy Rogers, Kit Carson, or The Lone Ranger fighting off the bad guys from behind big rocks, then you know where we held our Winter Jamboree. And, yes, we would have our own mock gunfights among the rocks. To tell the truth, while it was fun, hollering "Bang!" just did not have the same effect as hearing the blanks being fired and seeing smoke come out of the barrel.

Most of us were city-dwellers, and being out in the cold was a novel experience. As we were all good scouts, we had our canteens filled with water. Rule number one: empty them at night. Nighttime temperatures dipped below freezing, and the few stout souls who defied this rule found out what happens when water freezes and expands. Their canteens were no more!

Rule number two: socks burn. Almost every camp out had a campfire for cooking and to sit around and tell ghost stories.

But when at the Winter Jamboree, it was also for warmth. At night there were only two relatively warm spots: your sleeping bag and the campfire.

The campfire was both a blessing and a curse. The side of you facing the fire was nice and warm, even hot at times, while the back was freezing. To combat the cold, scouts would put on extra pairs of socks to keep their feet warm. Sitting on their portable camp stools and resting their feet on the fire ring rocks, someone's socks would start burning. There would be this funny smell, and smoke would emanate from someone's foot that was too close to the flame.

Adults were not immune to this catastrophe by any means. While they usually kept shoes and boots on until hitting the hay, they, too, would rest their weary feet on the fire ring rocks. Instead of socks burning, the odd smell was from the soles of shoes and boots being scorched or melting. When they realized what was happening, they would jump and dance, much to our delight and laughter, as they tried to cool down their shoes and boots.

The first themed amusement park was Knott's Berry Farm. In fact, Walter Knott sold the land to Walt Disney for his Disneyland in Anaheim. Knott and his wife operated a very popular restaurant that would frequently have a long wait to get a table. To give his patrons something to do while waiting to get in, he built a ghost town. One could sit in a chair on a wall in this town, and water actually ran upstream! There was a large fire pit surrounded by covered wagons, open on the fire pit side. If you were walking through the town or preferred to just sit and wait, you could rest in one of the wagons. Occasionally, small concerts were provided on Fridays and Saturdays. At that time, all of this was free.

Knott operated Calico ghost town out near Victorville, out in the middle of nowhere. One road in, one road out, neither of which was paved. The town was two blocks along the one road. There was a general store where kids could get old-time candy. A newspaper shop where you could get your picture on a wanted poster or on a newspaper with the "Wanted: Dead or Alive!" headline. There was the jail, and the saloon, and a church. Chairs were on the walls. Not nailed, just resting on a wall. And, again, there was the running faucet where water ran uphill.

The Winter Jamboree had several activities. On this one, there was a hike to the newly opened Calico Ghost Town. It was just a ten-mile hike from the campsite. Our troop, along with a guide with a map, would make the trip on a Saturday morning. We gathered up our stuff, and two of the leaders set out in a pickup to meet us at the town and drive us back to camp.

Although the guide cautioned us against rattlesnakes, there wasn't much chance of seeing one. The nighttime temperatures were in the upper 20s, and daytime did not hit 40. Too cold for cold-blooded creatures to be meandering about. The hike was to take about two hours, depending on the trail you took. After more than an hour and a half on the walk, dad asked the guide how much further. "Just over that ridge, there," he said, pointing to a high point about twenty yards ahead.

Well, he was half right. The town was just over the ridge

and could be seen from our vantage point. There was one slight problem. There was a 200-foot crevasse in front of us, and it was another 200 feet across. To get down, we had to hike down a hillside of loose rock, cross a dry riverbed, and then hike up another hillside of loose rock.

As we stood there dumbfounded with the adults talking not too kindly to our guide, who had his head buried in his map, a car's engine could be heard in the distance. The adults were too preoccupied with the map to hear it, but the scouts all faced the direction from which the sound was coming.

Finally, the green pickup truck belonging to one of the other scout leaders came to a stop. "Hey, what are you doing way out here?"

"Following this map," dad answered sarcastically.

"Well, do what you want, but the trail to Calico turned left about a mile back. Everyone is waiting on you. Get in and let's go."

Everyone piled into the truck, except the guide who hiked back to camp alone, and within five or ten minutes, we were at Calico. We all got out our Brownie cameras and shot picture after picture. Dad gave me enough money to either get a newspaper or a wanted poster. I opted for the newspaper. When we got home, I showed mom the paper. There we were, dad and I pictured below the headline, "Wanted: Dead or Alive!"

“Be Prepared” is the motto of the Boy Scouts. And on camping trips, this meant being prepared for almost any catastrophe: minor or major. It also meant be prepared to rely on nature for your next meal.

16

Shoes of the Fisherman

SHOES OF THE FISHERMAN

Frank was never really involved in the lives of his children. His relationship with Earl was strained from the beginning having missed the first three years of Earl's life. Copping with coming home from a living nightmare in the Pacific and trying to fit into the routine and bond between mother and son established during his absence. With many GIs coming home in the same situation, and all of them needing homes and jobs and a sense of security.

Frank and Earl did build a relationship as Frank taught his son about the things he knew. Construction and electrical wiring were at the core. Earl was a natural and enjoyed the time he and his dad spent in the garage/workshop.

Little League had an age limit. When Frank noticed Earl had both the talent and the desire to play organized baseball, Earl had aged out. There was a relatively new league for older boys, Pony League. Earl earned a spot on the Lightnings as first-baseman and relief pitcher. Frank helped coach both Earl and the team.

Earl was invited to join the Boy Scouts, and Frank became

Assistant Scout Master. When I became old enough, he joined also. Earl was a natural and eventually worked his way up the ladder to Life Scout, one step below Eagle. Then for reasons I never fully understood, Earl dropped out, and just as I earned Star Scout, one below Earl, dad took us both out of scouting.

Merle Haggard would write a song about the biggest river in San Bernardino County, Kern River, which has always been special to me. The song was OK, and it was a big hit for Haggard. Kern River was the site of the last camping trip dad, Earl, and I took as a scouting family.

The camping trip was in April when the days were warm and melted the mountain snow. Some of them were not familiar with snowmelt or what it did to the river. Because of the mild weather, we didn't sleep in tents but out under the stars. My patrol set up our campsite about six feet from the edge of the river. Overnight, the snowmelt from the previous afternoon reached our campsite. The problem was the river's width extended by about fourteen feet, seven feet on each side of the river. About three in the morning, the bank of the river was beginning to reach our sleeping bags. Half asleep and somewhat wet from the rising river, we moved our sleeping bags closer to the others and about twelve feet from the rising river.

The river was deep but with a meandering current. It provided fresh drinking water. Several of the scouts used their air mattresses as floating devices as they played in the river. I was by far the skinniest of the scouts. I would say that I was the thinnest, but that would presume I had meat and muscle on my bone. All I knew was that during the physical fitness test, where we had to weigh in, I was not the smallest scout. I was, however, the lightest one. This really did not matter until it came to Kern River. Snowmelt is cold. When I put my feet into the water, they literally froze. The muscles tensed, and I could neither wiggle my toes nor walk without some assistance. I think my dad thought I was a weakling.

When we did the fishing merit badge, I did a pretty good job with the mechanics. I could fly-cast further than either my dad or brother. Because of my think fingers, I was pretty adept at tying flies. I never earned the merit badge because you actually had to go fishing. When the troop went fishing, I couldn't go. It was a father-son event, and lightning had sparked a fire, and dad was on the fire line at the time.

We rarely went on a real vacation. Most of the time, when dad took his vacation, he did something around the house or helped somebody else with their special project. One summer, however, long after we were out of scouts, dad asked if I wanted to go fishing. Planning on it, he bought me a new fishing rod and reel. We hopped into his new toy, a shiny red Chevy pick-up, and drove into the mountains above Azusa to the San Gabriel River. We had all of our gear and were ready for anything. We promised mom fish for dinner, and we would provide the fish.

For about five hours, we moved from spot to spot but never got a bite. We would be at one spot, and another fisherman would direct us to another spot where the trout were biting. At the end of the day, after promising mom fresh fish, we had nothing.

On the way up, we passed a trout farm. This was a place

with a small pond stocked with good-sized, hungry trout. There was no actual fee for fishing, but you were charged by the pound for the fish you caught. After less than an hour, we had caught a half-dozen trout, which was more than enough for dinner. We paid the man and headed home.

"Not a word to your mother," dad admonished.

I'm not sure if dad spilled the beans or if we left some of the paper we wrapped our fish when we put them into the creels, but she knew they were not river trout.

"So, how was it fishing at the farm?"

I looked at dad. He raised his arms and shoulder in a questioning manner.

"I do not know. Dad and I spent almost all day at the river fishing" and headed off to bed.

Dad winked and gave me the OK sign.

Dad never came to any of my school functions. Whether they were French Club operas, PTA Shakespeare, or Orchestra performances, mom came by herself. Dad, I did one more thing together.

During my senior year, we moved to a new house in West Covina, about ten miles south of Azusa. It was not a brand new house, and when they built it, they used a lot of aluminum wire. This was common since copper was in scarce supply first for World War II, and to a lesser extent through the mid-50s and the Korean War. Now that copper wire was more plentiful, or maybe he got 'scraps' from work, we rewired the house during Easter vacation. Dad would undo sockets and switches and attach the copper wire to the aluminum. He would then disappear. At some point, he would holler, "OK," and he would pull the aluminum wire, and I would feed the copper wire. When all of the wire was pulled, I helped him tie the new wiring into the service panel. On some short pulls, I got to pull the wire while he fed it. It was hard work, and it was fun. Most of all, I enjoyed working with my dad on a project he enjoyed doing.

"Shoes of the Fisherman" was a book and movie about the Pope. Shopping for shoes with me was an adventure. My shoes were all leather, and I had many allergies. I would sneeze so much when buying shoes, my parents called me "Sneezy." But the most fun with shoes involved taking them off, running and sliding across the hardwood floors.

17

No Shoes on the Gym Floor

NO SHOES ON THE GYM FLOOR

In the late 50s and early 60s, there was not much to do on the weekend that did not potentially get you into some serious trouble. Fast-food restaurants were relatively rare, and so you could not go hang out. They existed in comic books and on television, but not in small towns such as Azusa. The drive-in was always an option if, and it could be a big if, you went to the drive in to watch the movie. We've all seen pictures of teens at the movies with windows so steamed up you can't see the side-view mirror, let alone the big screen a couple of hundred feet away.

During the summer, we would play streetball. You put something down, and that is home plate. Somewhere down the street, we put something else down, and that was second base. The light pole on the right was first base, and a designated spot on the left was third base. This was fun and good for a couple of hours of entertainment, providing you did not live on a busy street where you were constantly getting out of the way of cars. The second problem was the pop-up. High enough and hard enough, and there was a possibility that the first base went dark and it covered the diamond with glass. Game over.

We held Football games on the lawn. In our neighborhood, if one house had its driveway on the left side of the house, another had it on the right, allowing for combining the two yards for a single playing field. There were fewer problems with either cars driving down the street or balls hitting the streetlights.

That was pretty much the extent of our outside entertainment. Television broadcasted only a handful of channels, and nothing was on demand. Video games were not yet invented, but we did play board games. Sometimes, we would go for a night ride, but that could be problematic if your bike did not have some type of headlight. Parked cars were often dark, heavy, and potentially dangerous. None of that stopped the truly adventurous bike rider!

Once or twice a year, schools would have a record hop. Students come in and take their shoes off. They generally held dances in the gymnasium. Most of us wore hard, leather-soled shoes that damaged or destroyed the varnished vanish on basketball court floors. We actually learned how to dance in junior high, where dancing was part of the physical education curriculum. The dance segment was in the spring, and at the end of the grading period, eighth-graders would have a sock-hop for an hour or two after school.

Although the latest rock-inspired dances meant you never knew who you were actually dancing with, the slow dances required physical contact – but not too much. The chaperone's job was to ensure that they could see light between the dancers during the slow dances. If not, the chaperone, depending on whether a man or a woman, would place a hand on one of the dancers' stomach and gently remind them to separate a little.

By high school, those dancing slow dances were 'involved.' They were often a couple, and as long as hands remained visible, not a whole lot was said. The sexual revolution had not yet arrived, and unwanted pregnancies were difficult for everyone involved. They expelled girls from school, and they ostracized boys. The parents of the unfortunate couple wound up with problems of their own. So, no one really thought an unexpected family would result from a slow dance.

Dress codes were both conservative and strict. Boys could wear jeans or slacks, and, except for physical education, button-down shirts were the norm. Girls wore skirts or dresses with petticoats, with never a knee showing. Blouses or sweaters with minimal skin showing. Hair was short, and while bleaching had become a fad among some. Most schools would not allow it. In fact, Jack was sent home for bleaching his hair. Mom and dad had to go up to school and convince them Jack's hair was sun-bleached, which it was. Jack had naturally light brown hair; the top got lighter as he spent more time outside. My hair was more blonde, and if it got lighter the longer I stayed outside, no one noticed.

A record producer for a major record company, Martin Moore, moved into the community. His daughter complained that the "boondocks," as she referred to her new home, were too backward compared to the Hollywood area they recently moved to. Listening to his daughter complain and talking to school and community leaders, he came up with a novel idea. What about a teen club? The club would hold a dance at the National Guard Armory every weekend. He would get a couple of DJs to emcee the show and allow local bands to perform.

Everyone agreed it would be a good idea.

"I'm going to put the kids in charge," he told the leaders, who collectively gasped in disbelief. "Look, adults will be there, but let the kids make it their club. They can sell tickets, be the DJ, do a security check to ensure doors are locked and closed, and they can help run the concession stand."

He organized The club under the general name, ATC. Because the first club was in Azusa, we assumed it was the Azusa Teen Club. However, Moore indented to open more than one and said the initials stood for "A Teen Club," which eventually grew into "Associated Teen Clubs."

There was a record-only sock hop on Fridays and a full-blown dance on Saturdays with live music. As the club grew, Moore recognized that junior high students needed a similar venue. They relegated Friday nights to junior high students, with senior high students still in charge. The Saturday night sock hops featured some bands such as "The Tartans," who had released a record on a small, independent label and had received airplay, to "The Sliders," a pretty good band – they all had to audition – but had not yet acquired a recording contract.

The Boogie Boards from Hermosa Beach became the favorites and soon became the house band. They played a minimum of two weekends a month and were free to play other school sock hops and proms. When the Boogie Boards weren't playing, other bands stepped in. Between live sets, one of us would play DJ. We also ensured the microphones were on, and we worked the simple lightboard—three toggle switches. Up and the lights were on. Down and they were off. There was no in-between.

One of the DJs from Los Angeles was there when the Tartans played and got them signed to a major record. One side of the record was an instrumental titled "Accidental." On the flip side, a vocal called "Let's Go, Joe," was the side the band was promoting. However, the instrumental got them their record contract, and that's the side that was pushed. It was their first and only top 10 hit peaking at number 4.

Marijuana had been introduced into the music scene. One night while playing a high school dance in Anaheim, a couple of the members got high during the show. They stumbled around, had difficulty focusing on their music, and fell through a backdrop that was to be used for a high school musical production the following week. The whole incident was costly to the group. They lost their contract with the record company on a moral's clause, had to pay to replace the backdrop, which cost more than what the band took in during a month of sock hops. In the end, they were essentially banned from most high schools. The band never recovered, and their album would not be released except as a nostalgia item decades later.

I was on the security committee and walked around the building every half hour to make sure no one propped the doors open to allow non-paying guests to enter. We weren't really concerned. Anyone caught entering without paying or allowing others to enter without paying had their club membership terminated. In that, the police department was next door ensured there would not be any major conflicts.

There was a rotation of five or six rock/surf bands playing at the club. A number of major recording stars also performed. Some did their shows live, but most brought records they lip synched. I got to meet on my idols, a folk-pop recording artist from Seattle. One major concern happened when a major R&B artist, Lou Rawls appeared. There were no black students in the area, and no one was sure how everyone was going to react. There was no problem and opened the door to many more R&B artists to appear. One coup was Gene Pitney. He appeared on Saturday and then performed at the Oscars on Sunday. His theme to "The Man Who Shot Liberty Vallance" was up for an Academy Award.

At the end of the year, Moore took the committee members on a free trip to Disneyland, the newly opened amusement park operated by Walt Disney. At that time, you bought a book of tickets with multiples of four. We had a twelve-ticket book. Rides were assigned ratings from "A" for attractions such as animatronic presentations, to "E" tickets for rides along the Amazon or for driving on the highway of tomorrow." We also received some spending money, a set of Mickey Mouse Ears, and our pictures in the paper.

By the end of the second year, two more ATC sock hops were operating. Membership were interchangeable and when a major recording artist was appearing at one club, it would not be unusual for a large number of members from neighboring clubs to attend.

Using his connections between a local radio station and a movie studio, Moore decided to make a movie of the club. The Boogie Boards were signed to do the music and won a recording contract with a major record label. Jack and I were in the movie, and it took six weeks to film, usually after the Saturday night dance.

Before they released the movie, his record company fired Moore. He lost most of his contacts, had some marital problems, and everything collapsed. Before the ATC organization disappeared, the movie appeared on a local television station as a documentary. The movie was well-received, but the movie's limited success was not enough to save Moore's career or continue the ATC concept. There is only one copy of the movie, and it has never been shown beyond that one time on television.

Nancy Sinatra would become famous for "These Boots Are Made for Walking," and Joe South sang "Walk a Mile in my Shoes." I did not have any boots but shoes I did have. And took Joe South at his word and walked a mile – and then some, in my shoes.

18

Walk a Mile in my Shoes

WALK A MILE IN MY SHOES

Every student in high school during the 50s and 60s had to take physical education every year. My high school had a physical education period at the end of the day reserved for athletes. I was called many things growing up, but never an athlete. Yet, the only physical education period available to me was the last period of the day because of my academic schedule. Thus, I became an athlete.

For a male athlete, there were two options available. There was football. I had a couple of problems with this option. First, I was five-eight and 118 pounds. No amount of padding was going to give me enough bulk to block anything. I was not tall enough, fast enough, or coordinated enough to play a linebacker or quarterback. Besides, you had to try out, and besides, football season had already begun.

The other sport was cross-country. There were no tryouts, and everyone who came out was on the team. All you had to do is run and finish the three-mile course in under an hour. That I figured I could do, so I became a member of the cross-country team. At the time, I had no idea what cross-country was, but I learned very quickly.

Today, it is possible to buy a light-weight pair of shoes for whatever you want to do. There are shoes designed and built specifically for walking, running, cross-training, etcetera, etcetera, etcetera. However, in 1962 you had two options. You either had low cut tennis shoes or high top basketball shoes. Both were made of canvas and had rubber soles. By today's standards, they would have weighed the proverbial ton! I opted for the relatively lighter low-cut shoes.

There was a fenced-in field that was part of the schoolyard. Besides the grass, it was home to the football team's practice field and had a baseball diamond. It also was where the spring track meets were held, so there were areas for pole vaulting, long jump, and high jump. Most of the days, we practiced by running laps around this field.

Once we had gotten used to running on a flat surface, we moved to the Foothill Nursery. The nursery had a two-lane road running through the center of the nursery. As the name states, it was at the base of the hills at the San Gabriel Mountains base. The last quarter of a mile was at a significant incline. When we ran at the nursery, it was more about endurance than time. Our goal was to run up the hill, full tile, ten times each practice. I can say with pride that as practices progressed, I was no longer the slowest one on the team. I was never the fastest, but I was no longer the slowest.

I learned that if I could find a spot at the front of the mob, I could finish with a pretty respectable time. If I found myself at the back, I was mentally defeated, and my time reflected it.

To earn a letter in the sport, you had to run a qualifying meet within a specific time. With one meet to go, I found myself under the specified time for the first time. I was ecstatic. I was not an athlete, but I had just lettered in cross-country!

Wrong! When the list of those earning a letter was posted, Bruce Stoneman was not one of the names listed. I asked the coach about the lack of recognition.

"The last qualifying time was dropped by 15 seconds," he explained.

"Why didn't you tell me?"

"Simple, I didn't think you had it in you to meet the time needed to letter. I didn't see the point of telling you of the change."

That night, I had to retract my announcement that I was the first to letter in a school sport in our family. Truthfully, I don't think my parents actually believed I was letterman quality. The real bummer was I was within five seconds of the new lettering time! Had I known, I might have been able to earn that letter.

When I said that everyone had to take physical education, that was not exactly true. There was an alternate activity. Junior Reserve Officer Training Corps, JROTC. Fred Williamson, a good friend of mine, was in JROTC, and they marched in formation, in faux army uniforms and fake rifles. He was taller, heavier, and probably, at least in his mind, more coordinated than I was, and we would have friendly arguments over which was more beneficial: JROTC or cross-country.

In the fall of junior year in high school, President John F.

Kennedy lamented on the lack of physical stamina in the day's youth. He appointed actor Arnold Schwarzenegger as head of the youth physical fitness program. The two of them decided that every teen should be able to walk fifty-miles in one day. This became the buzz around the school for weeks. I was invited to go with some friends on this fifty-mile walk. I was not going to go then Fred challenged me. He said that he was in better shape and that I would never make it.

I told my mom, and she told my dad. He laughed and thought little of the idea. Chuck Jameson had just gotten a new Ford Falcon and drove from Azusa to Rancho Cucamonga from the police station. He found the newspaper office there, and they said they would be open until three that afternoon. He drove back and talked to the desk sergeant at the police station, and it was all arranged. We met on a Monday after school. We had a slip of paper. The police station in Azusa would sign the paper when we left and returned. That would be the official time. The newspaper in Cucamonga would stamp and sign the paper showing that we had been there and at what time. The walk would take place that Saturday. We would leave the police station at midnight and get back when we got back.

Mom was encouraging dad not so much. My bedroom had a separate entrance, so I could come and go without going through the house. At 11:00, I left the house and headed to the police station. It was a five-mile walk, and I took my time. I waited at the park near the station until I saw my friends show up. We all went inside, got our papers signed, dated, and stamped, and we were off. In military time, it was zero hundred hours.

I had one pair of tennis shoes, and they were in my locker at school for physical education. The rest of the time, we wore leather-soled loafers or lace-up oxfords. Today, I had on my lace-up oxfords for my trek into history. These were heavy and not particularly flexible, but it was we were all used to. None of us had tennis shoes on our feet for our walk. It just never entered our minds.

After walking for just over an hour, we were in the neighboring city of Glendora. About five minutes past the city limit sign, two police cars converged on us, lights flashing and very official. While crime was not a significant issue, the sight of five boys walking along a busy highway in the middle of the night was a concern that had to be addressed.

There was a car in front of us and a car behind us. Maybe they thought we were going to make a break for it.

"What's going on, guys?" the first officer asked.

"We're walking to Cucamonga," we offered in unison.

"And why would you want to do that?"

We looked at each other for a second or two. Then I said, "President Kennedy challenged all youth to walk 50 miles in a day. So, that's what we are doing. We left from the Azusa police department at midnight."

The two officers looked at one another. The obviously junior officer in the car behind us went and got on his radio. We stood there in silence while all of this transpired.

"They're O.K.," said the junior officer. "They checked in

with them when they left, and they'll be sticking to 66 all the way."

"Well, I don't know that I'd be walking 50 miles for the heck of it, but you all are a lot younger. Be careful and have a safe walk. We'll see you on the way back." We all shook hands. They got into their cars and left. Throughout the night, we were under constant surveillance by the police. There would be a honk as they passed us off from one jurisdiction to the next. This continued until about seven in the morning when the sun was well up.

All night convenience stores, all-night gas stations, and a plethora of fast-food joints were nowhere to be found as we walked along the highway. We assigned each of us something to bring. A former Boy Scout (always prepared, you know), I had my trusty canteen. It is was a community thing. We freely shared our canteens without concern about germs (or cooties)! Others had sacks with cookies and chocolate bars.

Nature called during the night, which meant finding a friendly bush that needed some unpurified liquid. This also had to take care of this between drive-byes by the police. Once the sun was up and gas stations opened, we could use a real bathroom. They also had vending machines, and we could get a coke (a euphemism for a soft drink, we called "pop." Coke referred to the style of beverage and not the brand). They also had water fountains so we could refill our canteens.

Somewhere between 8 and 9 in the morning, we found the Cucamonga Times and checked in. One by one, we presented our little slips of paper. They stamped it with the date and time, then signed it. They also stamped the paper's name on the sheet we handed to verify we had been there.

We were laughing and joking that we had made it half-way, and now for the return trip. We were tired and hungry, and the only place we found we could get something to eat, which had been scoped out before, was a McDonalds'. For less than a half-dollar, we could purchase a cheeseburger, fries, and a coke. We sat in the restaurant, talked, and wondered if anyone else has made progress. There was at least one other group, a JROTC group, also making the journey. We hadn't seen or heard from them.

After about a quarter-hour, it was time to head home. It was during daylight, and the air was considerably warmer than when we had left. This slowed us down, and fatigue was beginning to set in.

On the way out, we had walked pretty much like one cohesive unit. On the way back, we began to separate, and I was in the lead group. We had to stop periodically and wait for the stragglers to catch up. When we hit Glendora, it was about 4 in the afternoon. We had been walking 16 hours, and some could barely keep going. My four friends elected to stop at the McDonalds, use the payphone to call home, and call it quits.

I was pretty much doing this against my parent's wishes, so I did not see calling home as an option. I decided to press on by myself. I was within fifteen miles of the finish line, and I left them at McDonald's waiting for rides.

Just as I reached the Azusa city limit, a car with two of my travelers stopped to ensure I was O.K., and offer me a ride home. I said, "No, thank you. I'll make it. It's only a few more miles." They left, and I pressed on. I lied when I said I would call my parents from the police station, so I didn't have to walk home.

I reached the station at 5:10 pm—seventeen hours and ten minutes after I had started. The round trip was actually 52 miles. I still had another five miles to go before I got home. I stopped outside the Azusa Herald newspaper office and looked at the paper rack. A man was at the door, smoking a cigarette and watching me.

"What's going on?" he asked and offered a puff of smoke and a smile.

"I just finished a 50-mile walk," I said. The strategy was planned. It was my chance to make my parents proud and get my picture in the paper as proof that I had completed the trip.

"Come on in and tell me about it."

I spent about fifteen minutes sitting and resting my weary legs. He took my story down, took a few pictures, and promised it would be in the next issue. True to his word, there on the front page was my mug shot, my shoeless feet resting on the desk next to my lace-up oxfords.

By the time I got home, I had walked just over 60 miles. I literally collapsed when I got to my yard and crawled to the back of the house. Our hot water heater was in a closet on the back porch. We kept a spare key to the back door on top of the heater.

I lifted myself up, got the key, opened the door, put the key back, and crawled to the bathroom. I filled the tub with hot water and just sat there. I got out, made it out to my bedroom, and climbed into bed.

I got up the next morning, ready to tell my parents about my adventure. Apparently, I had already shared it with them.

Dad said, "We had gone to the store, and you were home when we got back. You were already in bed and asleep. We woke you, and you sat up and told us all about the walk. We're proud of you, son."

"Your eyes were puffy and shut closed the whole time," mom reported.

"Man, you looked terrible," Jack opined.

When I got to school on Monday, no one really believed I had made the entire trip, except my four walking buddies, who felt confident I had finished the challenge. However, they were not with me at the end. The Azusa Herald came out on Wednesday, and I was the celebrity of the day on Thursday. The principal even acknowledged what I had accomplished during morning announcements. Fred and the others who had chided me on Monday sang a different tune on Thursday.

"Hey, Fred," I called as we passed in the courtyard. "How long did it take you?"

"I found out I have a bad heart and had to call it quits after 15 miles." Fred blushed and quickly left for his JROTC class.

The celebrity status lasted a few days, and we all settled back into our daily routine. I was still in the athletic PE period, despite my begging my counselor to change my schedule. They assigned me the hundred-yard dash, which was not good. I could do distances, but slower than molasses in short runs.

My legs were never the same after my 50-mile trek. I offered to be a manager but was told that would not satisfy my

PE requirement. I was always last and the butt of jokes from the other team members, so I quit going. My PE grade for the next report card was an F. Yep, I failed physical education. I was one of three who failed that quarter. The other two? Well, they failed everything because they were constantly cutting school.

My parents were sympathetic. My counselor was surprised and changed my schedule, so I did not have athletics anymore. I guess she realized I was telling the truth when I said I was not an athlete. I got a B the next grading period, which suited me just fine.

My family moved my senior year, and I did not graduate from Azusa. My claim to fame is that I was truly one in a thousand. Between the two high schools I attended, there were just over a thousand students. I am the only one in the class of 1964, from either school, to walk fifty miles in one day.

After walking for more than seventeen hours, Azusa was the end of the line, in more ways than one.

19

At the End of the Line

AT THE END OF THE LINE

We lived about two miles from our high school. Each year the school district sets the boundaries of the school bus routes. Sometimes, we were in, and sometimes we were out. If we were in, the bus stop was at our end of the street or a block over. Other times, it was on our street but at the other end of the block. If we were out, we would walk whatever distance it was to the nearest bus stop. This was a fifteen-minute walk at the most. It was in front of a stone house, across the highway from the local rock and gravel company.

Jack and I would walk down to the bus stop and wait for it to arrive. Although it was required that everyone is seated. Simultaneously, on the bus, the driver seldom waited until that status had been achieved before starting on down the road. Our stop was full, and if you were lucky, a friend had saved you a seat. Otherwise, it was potluck. It might be someone you knew and liked, but just as often, it was either a stranger or someone that was not on your 'friend' list.

It took about fifteen minutes to get to school. Our school was on an eight period day, but you didn't take eight classes.

You took five or six classes, so you might not have to go to class as soon as the bus arrived. It also meant you might have to wait about an hour before the bus came in the evening. Regardless of how many classes you had, you often had a period on certain days where you did not have a class. Science classes had lab periods twice a week. When you didn't have a class, you could sit in one of the courtyards, go to one of the snack windows, or go to the library. The time was your own.

After school, I would often walk home with Chad, Ricky, and a few others, both boys and girls. We walked as a group, and when we reached one of the other's houses or street, they went home. I lived the furthest, and the last half-mile was me and my vivid imagination.

Riding the bus home was not all that unpleasant except for two sections of town. Because of the staggered school day, the bus ride home was less crowded. It was easy to find a seat for you and a friend, or even to have a seat alone as you contemplated the complexities of the world around you.

The first stops were north of the city at the base of the mountains. This was one of the unpleasant parts of the route. At the base of the mountains was the Foothill Dairy with hundreds of noisy cows and a smell no city-boy could appreciate. Most of us were unaccustomed to the smells and sounds of a working farm, dairy or otherwise. We were ecstatic when those unfortunate kids got off, and the bus moved on.

Lucky Lager Beer was a regional beer brand and had a brewery in town. That was the other smelly parts of the trip. No one was quite sure why the brewery was so aromatic, but if you were lucky, you only had your senses assaulted for a few minutes. Most of the time, however, we were not that lucky. About the time the bus was rolling through, a freight train would come passing by. There we were, windows open, and our sense of smell was annihilated as this always long and slow-moving train went through.

Finally! The train is passed, the gates are up, and we are moving. I am the fifth and last stop after that. "Thanks, and see ya later, Mr. Brown," was the usual comment as we disembarked. Jack was on the first bus route. I was on the last one. As I got off the bus, I noticed bits of cloth lying on the road. The fabric was a plaid, the same as one of my favorite shirts. Jack rode the bus to school that morning. Because I didn't have to be there until the third period, I walked and left before Jack, and I did not see what shirt he had on.

There were bits, and pieces of what I was convinced was a shirt along the roadway home. And not just any shirt, my favorite shirt. Although we were not twins, we could easily wear each other's clothes. Because I was slightly taller, it was easier for Jack to wear a shirt of mine, whereas his shirts were a bit small and tight-fitting.

When I got home, there was my favorite plaid shirt, or what remained of it, on my bed. It was torn to shreds. One sleeve was missing, as was one of the breast pockets. The other was literally holding on by a thread.

"Jack! What happened," I demanded, holding up what was left of my favorite shirt.

He glanced up from what he was doing and looked at what was left of my shirt. "Oh, that," he said. "I got a ride home, and your shirt got torn in the process."

"What do you mean you got a ride home?" I queried.

"Simple, I got a ride home on a cement truck. When he came out of the rock quarry, I jumped on. He saw me and pulled over, stopped to look. I was off by then and waving at him. Then when he started up, I got back on. It was a heck of a ride!"

"And the shirt?" I said, getting angrier by the minute

"I stayed on until he got to Vernon. There he had to stop, and I hopped off and walked home. Unfortunately, I lost my footing, and your shirt got caught on something; I fell, and the shirt got ripped to hell. Bummer!" Jack was the only one of the three boys to routinely curse.

Mom came home from work and came into the bedroom while I was still holding the shirt.

"What happened?" she asked in surprise.

Before I could say anything, Jack blurted, "Flag Football." He then looked at me, defying me to contradict him.

"Are you alright?" She inquired, walking over to and inspecting Jack

"Yeah, just some scratches and some dirt and stuff. See?" he said, pointing to a couple of scratches around his left elbow.

"Next time, take your shirt off. This thing is ruined," and walked out of the room with the damaged shirt.

"Don't even . . ." Jack said, raising a fist, and walked out of the room.

In high school, I took French. I was in college prep classes and we had to take a foreign language and so I chose French. Others with an eye towards medicine took Latin, and those with a flair for engineering took German. But there is more to a language than the words. There is the culture behind the words and traditions. If you do not know the culture, speaking fluidly in the foreign language does not help.

20

Geoffrey Chaucer - Esque

GEOFFREY CHAUCER – ESQUE

One illusion of being passionate about music is the belief anyone can make it. While in high school, using the contacts I made while with the teen club, I began writing music. I was 15 when I first submitted my first song, and more than a hundred rejections later, I still have not written a song that has been published, let alone recorded.

Or, have I?

I realized that a lot of what I was writing was immature junk. I don't think that even if I had a band of my own, I would record what I had written. So, I decided to tackle a more mature subject: the anniversary of a break-up between a man and a woman. I really never had a girlfriend, so my vision of what it would be like to still miss someone after a year was pure fiction.

In the 50s and 60s, writing music was a risky business. Not that you could get in trouble, but if you weren't careful, you could have your song stolen with little or no recourse. To copyright a song cost $25.00 and a form from the Library of Congress. You also had to provide a copy of the song and since there were no copiers. It meant copying it over by hand. This was also true when submitting the song to prospective agents and publishing companies. They wanted a copy of the song, so I spent a lot of time re-copying junk that I knew, deep down, would never be published.

Then, I got sloppy and was naïve when someone said they would help me. I met a disc jockey who had ties with record companies and music publishers from my teen club days. I sent him a song. I sent it without first copyrighting the song. If you didn't have the money to file the paperwork, you could mail yourself a copy of the song, registered mail, and keep it sealed until and unless it became necessary to prove you wrote the song.

I didn't file the official forms, nor did I the money to send me a copy by registered mail. I just sent it to the disc jockey, who never responded. This, in and of itself, was not unusual as publishers receive hundreds of unsolicited manuscripts, and except for the biggest, they could not afford to send receipts or rejection notices to every composer or lyricist.

A pop recording star released his latest song. I had heard it on the radio and really liked it. I went down to Whites, a membership-only department store to which my parents had recently purchased a membership. I bought the record, and while standing in line, I flipped the record over to see what was on the other, or "B" side. The song that was there just because there had to be a second song. Imagine my shock when I saw the disc jockey to whom I submitted the song wrote the song. To make things worse, there was a single word difference in the title. I took the record home and immediately put it on the record player. Instead of playing the "A" or hit side, I flipped the record over. I also dug out my handwritten lyric sheet. The song being sung was word for word what I had written, save the one word difference.

I was always tilting at windmills and living a Walter Mitty life, dreaming of making it big as a musician, songwriter, actor/director, and my parents did not always take my efforts seriously. Mom was more supportive than dad, but it was their lack of belief in me that I did not risk spending the money to either copyright or send it registered mail.

I showed mom my lyric sheet. "That's nice, honey," she said dismissively. After some persuasion, I got her to sit down and listen to the record and follow my lyric sheet. I am not sure how much she believed in me.

"It's a big record company, he's a big star, and you are . . . well, you are you. What do you think will happen?" The record sold a million copies, and the disc jockey got paid $10,000 for a song we both know he didn't write.

I continued writing, but more practically. I enjoyed writing stories for English classes, and sometimes, just for the fun of it. For whatever reason, when I transferred to my new high school during my senior year, they put me in a college-prep class that was team-taught by an English teacher and a history teacher. Either you had English fifth period and history sixth period, or vice versa. They taught the two classes in a round building with an accordion-fold wall separating the two classes. Once a month, the wall opened up, and for two hours, we were all together.

Between the two English classes, there were three Japanese

foreign exchange students. We bonded easily and early since we were all in the same boat. We were in a strange school without a lot of friends. If it took me an hour to do my English homework, it would take them up to three because of their limited English proficiency.

The class began a unit of the Canterbury Tales, and we would, over the course of a week, read and then discuss a tale from the travelers. Dr. Ewing assigned us to write an original Canterbury style tale. I chose to tell the tale of an artist. After spending an hour with the three of them in the library after school one day, I helped them decide on a character for their tale. We would meet regularly after school so I could help them. I got my story written the first night and gave it to them as a model. They still had difficulty comprehending since the form was foreign to them. I decided to go the extra mile. Over the weekend, armed with their notes on their characters, I wrote their tale for them. On Monday, I gave each of them their tale with the instructions they copy it over in their own handwriting.

When Friday came, and we had to turn the stories in, the two in my class looked at me. I smiled and nodded for them to turn them in. Hesitantly, they put their papers on the stacks. It was a long weekend waiting until we got our grades on Monday. Would the teacher know that I had written the three stories for my new Japanese friends, and if he did, what would he do? The four of us met in the library Monday after school to compare grades. I received a 94; each of them had grades from 82 to 88. As it turns out, they had altered slightly my tale written for them, thus possibly accounting for the different grades.

A few months later, we got our final report card of the year. Seniors got out of school ten days ahead of everyone else to prepare for graduation. As I was leaving for the last time, the teacher called me to his desk.

"Stoneman, I have really appreciated having you in class this year. You'll go far, I am sure."

"Thank you," I got out. Blushing and stammering along the way.

"I must say, I really enjoyed your Canterbury Tale." I looked at him, and he had a slight smile on his face.

"All four of them." He winked. "Your friends wanted me to know how you had helped them. They did not want you to get in trouble, but how appreciative they were of your willingness to help three strangers. They were equally surprised you wanted nothing in return."

I said, "Well, they were struggling, and I thought I could help. They're going back to Japan and will graduate from their home schools. I just thought it was the right thing to do."

He shook my hand, wished me well, and as I walked out the door for the last time, he said, "Stoneman! Really. Thank you." He returned the work on his desk, and I walked out the door.

Now what? I have graduated from high school without a real plan for the summer, let alone for the future. Then life happens!

21

I'm an Old Cow Hand

I'M AN OLD COW HAND

June of '64 could not come quick enough. It was my time to shine and be the first of the three boys to graduate from high school. Seniors took their finals a week earlier than everyone else, and that last week of school was getting ready for the big day. Being sunny California, our ceremony would be held outdoor at the football field. There were a myriad of other little things going on. Being Catholic, we had a baccalaureate service on Sunday. a senior breakfast on Monday, and a senior lunch on Wednesday. We received our cap and gowns on Tuesday and confirmed the spelling of our names. Thursday was dress rehearsal, and the big day was Saturday morning. We walked the length of the football field, and all 526 of our names were called—applause and cheers after each name.

By Monday morning, fun and games were over. Many had jobs lined up and went to work almost immediately. Some of us had college plans and went to a junior college over the summer or relaxed until the fall semester. A few enlisted in the armed services and were on their way to basic training.

I fell into the college-bound group. I had applied and been

accepted to a business college in Los Angeles, but classes would not start until the fall. In the meantime, my uncle secured me a position as a camp counselor at the Stanley Ranch Camp in the desert north of Los Angeles. It was similar to a Boy Scout or Girl Scout camp but was run by The Woodcraft Rangers. The WoodCraft Rangers were founded by naturalist Ernest Thompson Seaton. They are the oldest youth group in the country and a precursor to the much larger Boy Scouts.

The Woodcraft Rangers operated two camps. The dude ranch camp to which I was assigned, and a naturalist camp at Lake Arrowhead in the San Bernardino Mountains. We were hired for nine weeks over a ten-week period. We would have one week free during the camp sessions.

Regardless of which camp you were assigned to, all counselors met at Stanley Ranch. My uncle was an official with the organization and had to take some materials to the camp, so I rode up with him. We were all sizes, shapes, and colors. I became friends with Linda from Pomona and was a three-year veteran. She also had a sporty green MGB sports car. Some of the paperwork for campers assigned to Stanley was accidentally sent to Lake Arrowhead. Linda worked at the Arrowhead camp and volunteered to go retrieve the errant paperwork.

"Want to go with me?" she asked, looking straight at me.

“Me?”

She nodded affirmatively.

“Sure.”

We left at six the next morning. It was a three-hour drive and was warm already. The top was down, and I enjoyed the trip. We talked about everything from future plans to our families. She was a third-year biology major at Cal-State Irvine. His goal was to become a high school biology teacher like her mother. She did not rule out medical school, but the cost was worrisome to her. I shared that I was headed down the road to becoming a CPA eventually.

Actually, I lied. After I got admitted to the business college, I even took a bookkeeping class in high school. Hated it! It was boring, and my mind kept wandering. I managed a "B" out of the class, but that was more luck than talent.

When we got back to Stanley Ranch, the cooks had prepared a feast for all the counselors. We had pie for dessert. I only knew of two fruit pies, apple, and cherry, and this pie was definitely not a cherry pie.

"This is a really good apple pie,' I said to Linda.

She laughed and almost choked on the piece she had just put in her mouth. "This is not apple pie!"

"No? Then what is it?"

"Rhubarb."

I had never heard of rhubarb, let alone had any. We had rhubarb pie at least once a week, and it soon became my favorite.

One of the activities we were to do was take the campers on a horseback ride. Jimmy was the camp wrangler and agreed to take us, greenhorns, on a practice run. This was promised on Monday, and we kept being reassured that it would happen before the campers arrived on Sunday. I was nervous, to say the least. I had never been on, let alone ridden a horse. And they expect me to lead a group of kids on a horseback ride!

By Saturday, it was clear the training session with Wrangler Jimmy would not be taking place. Saturday evening, we met in the chow-hall to learn about our campers and the schedule of activities for the upcoming week.

We all had eight kids, and we were assigned to a camping area named for a western personality. I was assigned to Gabby Hayes (Roy Rogers sidekick on his television show). It rarely rained, and we slept under the stars. During the training, the guys slept under the stars while the female counselors slept in the bunkhouse.

"You are up first for the ride on Sunday afternoon," Jimmy told me. "Don't worry. I'll have you on Daisey. She sweet and knows the way. Just let her lead, and no one will ever know this is your first trip."

I wasn't so sure, but I did not have much choice, either.

At one-o'clock, the Gabby Hayes' assembled at the corral. Each boy sat atop the fence and watched as Jimmy brought Dancer, his own horse out. He explained how the horses were taken care of and took them through the steps cowboys took in saddling up their horses.

He brought Daisey out already saddled and had me come down and mount up. I sat atop Daisey and watched as each camper was brought out and mounted on a horse. He then opened the gate, said something to Daisey, and off we went.

At about half-way through the ride, we arrived at the Mushroom Tree. The tree, shaped perfectly like a mushroom, especially when viewed from a distance, seemed out of place. There was not another tree for several feet in any direction.

Jimmy was waiting there for us and had water and snacks for us.

"The legend of the mushroom tree," Jimmy began, "goes back to when only cowboys, cattle, and rattlesnakes ruled this area." Jimmy was a good story-teller and had the boys firmly in his hand as he explained the feud between cattle ranchers and sheep-herders erupted one morning.

"This tree is where Tom Snook, the shepherd, had his house. His family would come out the front door and picnic under this very tree," Jimmy said in a matter-of-fact tone. "Late in the afternoon, there was a gunfight, and Tom was killed." Jimmy paused for effect. "Tom's family fled to another shepherd's house and watched as their house was burned down, and the tree was badly damaged."

Jimmy took a moment to look each camper in the eye. "This tree has magical powers. In the morning, a miracle happened." Jimmy paused again. "This tree was seen to be completely undamaged by the night's fire. The branches that had been seen burning were not to be found."

Jimmy explained that each of the cattlemen involved in the raid on Tom's cabin mysteriously died or were injured. "Every one of them. Not a single man from that night escaped punishment for what they had done. And in the years since then, anyone kicking the tree or pulling off leaves has had to face the curse."

At that, most of the boys laughed and challenged what they had heard. Johnny, a shy little boy, sat there silently. Jimmy walked over to him and asked what was wrong.

“I did not really mean to, but I accidentally pulled off some leaves.”

"Thank you for telling me," Jimmy said calmly. "I'm sure the tree knows it was an accident."

“I am afraid.”

“Why?” asked Jimmy.

“My brother, Kenny, came last year. He pulled some leaves off the tree. The night he got home from camp, he fell out of bed and broke a tooth. I do not want that to happen to me."

Everyone heard the story, and it got quiet. Jimmy assured Johnny he would be alright, got everybody back on their horses, and headed back to camp as he cleaned up after the break.

Each night, there was a large campfire. Each campsite was charged with sandpainting a design around the fire circle, and tonight was our night. We were given instructions, powdered paint, and the boys painted the design. Tonight, it was a thunderbird. Each group got to tell something about what happened during the day. The Gabby Hayes' told of their horse ride, but not much about the Mushroom Tree.

Harold, the camp administrator, gave a welcoming speech and said a brief prayer. Then everyone was instructed to look at the hills, and a flaming arrow was seen. It shot through the dark sky and landed somewhere out of sight. The boys oohed and aahed at the view of the flaming arrow. Two counselors were stationed near the arrow's target to dowse the flame and prevent unintentional fires.

There was a small zoo, and non-venomous snakes, lizards, and tarantulas were kept. Boys were allowed to handle them.

There was a snake known as a red racer in the zoo. A boy from Roy Rogers' camp announced there were now two snakes. They had found a blue racer and placed it in the zoo.

"Nope!" It was a camper from the Lone Ranger camp. "The red racer ate the blue racer, and we are back down to one snake."

On Friday, the boys learned of the Indian tradition of painting stones and marking a good spot by stacking them. Then, when they passed this way next year, they knew it was a good spot. The boys spent Friday painting the rocks. They took them to the campfire, and after the ceremonies were finished, each camp took their rocks to a spot near where they were sleeping and placed them in a pile, signifying this was a good spot and they had fun during their stay.

The boys learned a lot of things during the week. They rode horses, played with the zoo animals, made different things, and had fun swimming. They also learned that there were consequences for their actions. If they were good during the day, they got more time in the pool or maybe an extra snack. If they were overly excited and slow to follow directions, they might not get as much time at the zoo as they would like. There were no promises or warnings. They just learned that things happened based on their actions.

Milestones mark the end of an era or a chapter in our life. It is a time of reflection and contemplation.

22

I Am Gone

I AM GONE

1960 was one of the most violent decades in American history. It was as if The Age of Innocence sent us a card saying, "I am gone!" In its place came the Age of Aquarius. Girls being sent home from school in 1960 for having a hemline above the knee were now baring it all in public, in magazines, in movies, and even on Broadway! We went from smoking cigarettes and cigars to smoking (and eating) marijuana or weed. There were heroin addicts primarily relegated to the "other side of the tracks" and skid row. Main-stream America was dealing with nicotine and alcohol addiction. By the end of the decade, we would be dealing with psychedelic and hallucinogenic drugs. More hard-core drugs such as cocaine were making their way into our society. It was a violent time that saw a president, his brother, and a civil rights leader assassinated. War divided our nation and our politics. Our President engaged in breaking and entering for political purposes.

There were times, to be sure when we were at our finest. The space race was heating up, and we eventually put a man in space, and we headed to the moon. What this meant to us as a nation and as a world would change how we live and think. From everyday appliances to clothing. From what we eat to how we prepare what we eat. From our clothing to our toys. The world was changing at break-neck speed, and it everything we could muster to hang on.

The most divisive element, and the only one to personally affect me, was Viet Nam. Too many young men whom I knew and worked with went to Viet Nam. Each week, the Navy published a newspaper, *The Navy Times*, and listed all of those killed since the previous issue. These boys that I knew and worked with were listed in the paper and came home in a box.

I served and was exempt from the draft. I managed to dodge the bullet and pretty much stayed out of harm's way. I did volunteer multiple times, but my then commanding officer denied each offer. My whole family dodged the bullet. Both brothers were on carriers and were involved in support of the conflict. Still, neither were actually involved in the war. Other families were not so lucky.

When I started college, I met a student who planned to take over his family's retail business. The draft was being talked about, and there were certain exemptions or deferments. One was being in college. So, this young man enrolled in the School of Business. Then the deferment was changed, and to be deferred meant following a specific career path. So this student changed from the School of Business to the School of Education because teachers met the deferment criteria. Then the government changed their mind again, and deferment applied only to married men. So he married his high school sweetheart and started a family, as the government changed their mind once again, and only married men with families would be deferred. Before he graduated, the government ended all deferments, and he was drafted. Today, his name is etched for eternity on a black marble wall.

To avoid being drafted, Martin enlisted in the Navy. However, it was not long before he was reassigned to the Fleet Marine Force and found his way to Viet Nam. He was a passenger on a helicopter when it crashed. His family was notified. He arrived home with the usual caveat that the family did not view the remains, and his family buried him.

Years later, a picture of an unidentified POW appeared on the cover of a national news magazine. If it was not Martin, it was his twin brother. After several weeks, the government determined that the picture was not that of Martin, but another previously identified POW.

The family did not have confidence in the government's conclusion and began looking into Martin's death circumstances. The body was exhumed and examined by a nationally recognized anthropologist. The family obtained records of the accident and death certificates of all those onboard. Despite the number of irregularities and discrepancies, the government would not waiver on their insistence that the body was that of Martin. The story of Martin was featured on a nationally broadcast, reality-based television show. Eventually, DNA identification had progressed to the point where a viable DNA identification was possible. A well-known and reputable DNA laboratory concluded the body was not that of Martin to a certainty greater than 99%. This information was given to the government. They released a statement that their DNA expert concluded that the body was Martin's to the same degree of certainty.

Television had moved from the studio to the community. The war was routinely broadcast live during the family's dinnertime, as well as images of violent protests and students being shot on campus. They were present at a national political convention and showed the arrest of seven protesters.

Singer Bob Dylan said it best with his song, "The Times They Are a-Changing." Change is inevitable. Change is neither good nor bad, a blessing or a curse. It just is. Where would I have been, and how would I have been changed without Earl's polio and teasing. What would I have done without Jack's ingenuity? How might my life be today if I had not learned the accordion and let so much music into my life?

At one point, Jack and my dad conspired to have me move my family from Texas back to California. If I had agreed, my life would be very different than it is today. Neither better nor worse, just different. By deciding to remain in Texas also changed my life. Unwilling or unable to comprehend why I would not jump at the opportunity to be physically closer to the family hurt my relations with the family.

The *Age of Innocence* was not always so innocent. Girls with unexpected pregnancies were left with few choices and were ostracized from the community. The school district removed the girl from school, and the families would be gossip and harassment. People were denied access to the basic qualities of life. All of this because of the color of their skin or the shape of their eyes. Stereotypes were prevalent in society and promoted on television and in movies.

How and where we are raised often determines how we live our lives. It also affects how we interact with others and how we raise our children. Many of us view our childhoods as a more-simple time. I am sure my parents raised us and instilled in us what they considered the best of their growing up. I know we have done that with our children. As I look back at my first two decades of life, many mistakes were made. There are things I could have and probably should have done differently. Looking back at the pictures of my life, I realize how much I have to be thankful. It has also allowed me to accept and be grateful for the changes, challenges, opportunities, and experiences that have followed.

Steve Wilcox is a retired schoolteacher, entrepreneur, and conference presenter. He received his B.S.Ed. from the University of Dayton and an M.Ed. from Miami University of Ohio. He also received a Mid-Management certificate from Tarleton State University in Texas. Mr. Wilcox has taught from 4th grade (substitute) to continuing education at the junior college level. His teaching experience has included urban, rural and he spent ten years working with incarcerated youth.

When not teaching, he operated a motivational business for industry, a mail-order motivational tape business, and ran his own insurance agency. He also worked as a road-side assistance coordinator for an OTC trucking company and wrote advertising copy for a local radio station.

Steve and his wife, Judy, have been married for 53 years. They have two children and two grandchildren. He and his wife reside in Hewitt, Texas.

CPSIA information can be obtained
at www.ICGtesting.com
Printed in the USA
LVHW082141090421
683732LV00037B/150

9 780578 824048